MW01107471

THIS BOOK BELONGS TO

ROGER S. BAUM

THE

OZ

ODYSSEY

Illustrated by
Victoria Seitzinger

The Overmountain Press

JOHNSON CITY, TENNESSEE

ISBN 1-57072-299-4

Inquiries should be addressed to:
The Overmountain Press
P.O. Box 1261
Johnson City, TN 37605

1 2 3 4 5 6 7 8 9 10

First Edition

To My Readers

We are on our way again, my Oz friends. Before I go much further, I want to send you all my love as we travel down the Yellow Brick Road together, a journey that includes love, wisdom, heart, and courage. I suppose life, if lived fully, will always be filled with these things. If it were not, it would be quite dull, to say the least.

Indeed, the Yellow Brick Road is more than just a road that takes us from one place to another, although the Yellow Brick Road does take us from Munchkin Land to the Emerald City and back. The real journey, for all of us, is what happens along the way. Therefore, I would like to take this opportunity to wish you well on your own adventure, and perhaps if I am lucky enough to meet you, we will share adventures together.

You will notice that this Oz adventure has three sections, each marked by its own color. The first section is red, the second is green, and the third is yellow. Don't let the colors fool you, though—it is one story.

Now, how about an explanation:

Red

Red is for the Red Brick Road. People have often asked me where the Red Brick Road leads. Though still a mystery, Dorothy discovers part of the answer when she and Toto take a shortcut off the Yellow Brick Road into a dangerous and fantastic land.

Green

Green is for the Oz Forest. The Lion, the Scarecrow, and the Tin Woodman follow Dorothy's trail off the Yellow Brick Road, where they must go through the wonderful Oz Forest to reunite with their friends.

Yellow

Yellow is for the Yellow Brick Road. Before they can get back to the Yellow Brick Road, the friends need to cross the Silver Bridge. Hopefully, the People of the Clouds can help.

Now you are on your way! Good Luck!

Fondly,
Roger S. Baum

Author's Note

As most of you know, Great-grandfather penned fourteen Oz books among his sixty-one works. Ruth Plumly Thompson authored nineteen additional Oz books.

As more and more works were developed, more and more inconsistencies arose, not only between the books themselves but between the books and the movie version as well.

None of these inconsistencies subtract from the many adventures. In the case of Oz, they add debate for those who like to discuss these things—they add to the fun of a national treasure.

So, I hope you will sit back and enjoy *The Oz Odyssey*.

List of Chapters

PART I

DOROTHY TAKES A SHORTCUT

The Land of Never Return

It had become a very long day for Dorothy and Toto. Gray clouds moved in, covering the Oz sky and threatening rain.

Dorothy had decided to travel off the Yellow Brick Road. She was late, and she thought she would save some time by cutting directly to the south toward Quadling Country, though she knew that leaving the Yellow Brick Road to take a shortcut through the unknown Oz Forest could be dangerous.

But her good sense left her when the rain clouds came. Besides, she did not wish to be late for her meeting with her friends the Lion, the Scarecrow, and the Tin Woodman.

Dorothy found a small pair of scissors in her sewing kit. She decided to use the scissors to carve an "X" on trees to mark her trail, in case she became lost and needed to backtrack.

Dorothy and Toto headed south through the mysterious forest, where they discovered new kinds of animals, flowers, and plants. One flower, for instance, was green and yellow with a red stem.

"Look, Toto," she said, "there's a purple squirrel."

THE OZ ODYSSEY

Dorothy held Toto so he wouldn't chase the small animal, as dogs are prone to do. Luckily, the purple squirrel quickly found an opening in some rocks and disappeared from sight.

Traveling off the Yellow Brick Road was very interesting! Soon, however, this colorful part of the forest was behind them.

Dorothy continued to mark their path. She had just started walking again after marking another tree with an "X," when she noticed a wooden sign that read:

STOP!

YOU ARE ENTERING

THE LAND OF

NEVER RETURN

Dorothy was surprised to find a sign in the middle of the forest. She hesitated, but she had come too far to turn back now. Her determination won out. She picked up Toto and walked cautiously past the wooden warning sign.

Suddenly she noticed a tiny lady directly in front of her. The lady stood perfectly still. She was only nine inches tall, at the most. She wore a thin smile and was dressed like a princess.

The tiny woman's small black eyes penetrated Dorothy with an intense stare. Her eyes were especially mysterious against her pale skin; they were further emphasized by her woven black hair, which reflected a silver sheen from a beam of bright sunlight that had somehow found its way through the forest canopy.

THE OZ ODYSSEY

The tiny woman's cheeks were pale, and her lips had a green tint. Silver sequins hemmed the black dress she wore, and green sequins rimmed her small black shoes. She carried a wand in her hand.

But something about the tiny princess gave Dorothy an uncomfortable feeling. She looked just like a toy doll.

A toy doll—of course, thought Dorothy. *That's what she is.*

She reached to pick up the doll, but it suddenly moved to avoid her outstretched hand.

"Don't touch me," the doll warned.

"Oh, my!" exclaimed Dorothy. "I am sorry. I thought you were a doll."

"No, I am not a doll," the tiny woman replied. "My name is Bekama. I am the leader of the Tinybits. And you are the famous Dorothy."

Surprised, Dorothy wondered how she knew her name.

"Why do you invade the land of Never Return?"

"This is not an invasion," Dorothy replied, puzzled. "It is only my dog, Toto, and me. We are traveling on our way through the south of Oz. We wouldn't invade anyone—"

"Well, nonetheless," interrupted Bekama, "you have disobeyed our warning sign and entered our land. So you have indeed invaded our territory."

Bekama's strong words astounded Dorothy, as she did not expect them to come from such a tiny, princess-like person. Dorothy towered over her.

"You see, if I allowed you to leave," Bekama continued, "you would tell others, and we would have more intruders coming to Never Return. Our little land would be overrun."

Just then, several other Tinybits joined Bekama, including five tiny soldiers and a tiny lady-in-waiting. Dorothy studied the guards; something about them seemed very familiar, though she didn't know what.

"Remember, Dorothy, we are not dolls," Bekama said firmly. "We know that our towns would be crushed by the many who would visit merely out of curiosity. They would crush our crops and our homes. Therefore, to guard our secret, you and your dog can never leave."

Dorothy could not believe her ears. "Can never leave?! Please let us go. We promise not to tell anyone. My friends are waiting for me. They will be worried if I do not arrive soon."

"I'm sorry, I cannot allow you to leave," repeated Bekama harshly.

Dorothy decided she could not wait any longer. "Let's run, Toto!" she yelled to her little friend. She turned quickly and ran back in the direction of the Yellow Brick Road.

Toto knew that something was wrong, so he ran very close to Dorothy.

"Run, Toto, run! We will prove that this is not a land of Never Return."

Dorothy spotted the mark she had made on a tree near the entrance sign to Never Return. She stopped for a moment and hurriedly picked up Toto. Then she quickly looked around for Bekama and the rest of the Tinybits.

They are so small, she thought, *they could hide anywhere. They could be watching us.*

"Let's go, Toto," Dorothy said. "We will follow our tree markings to the Yellow Brick Road." She took five more steps to the warning sign and found that she and Toto could not move forward. Something invisible blocked their way.

Dorothy couldn't see the barrier, but she could feel it. It felt like a rubber balloon. It pushed in like a rubber balloon but did not burst like a balloon might.

Dorothy walked back a few steps. She put Toto in her basket and then set the basket carefully upon the ground. She covered Toto with Auntie Em's checkered picnic cloth and left a place for him to see out.

Then she ran as fast as she could into the invisible barrier. This time it gave a little more, but it quickly snapped back, throwing her head over heels backward.

Dorothy landed hard on the forest floor. She narrowly missed her basket with Toto inside. Toto was so startled, he jumped straight up into the air and then ran to Dorothy.

Dorothy had just started to pick herself up off the ground, when Toto, in all his excitement, ran straight into her. She found herself flat upon the forest floor again, only now Toto was standing on top of her chest. He was licking her face, attempting to comfort her.

She quickly stood up, brushed off her dress, and assured Toto she was all right by petting the top of his furry little head.

Dorothy looked around. Something peculiar was happening. The forest trees seemed much taller than before. Indeed, everything appeared larger—except for Toto.

It's my imagination, she thought to herself.

Dorothy's thoughts turned to her friends. She worried that she would not appear in time for her meeting with the Lion, the Scarecrow, and the Tin Woodman. She also knew how concerned they would be if she did not arrive as expected. *My poor friends,* she thought. Dorothy was more concerned about her friends than herself.

She noticed that the forest shadows had grown longer as the Oz sun dipped toward the horizon. She picked up her basket. It felt larger and much heavier than before. Even the apple inside of it looked huge.

The apple had been given to her by one of the Apple Trees. As time passed, the trees had grown happy to see her, and they offered her an apple every time she walked by. But Dorothy didn't remember receiving an apple this big from the Apple Trees. In fact, she didn't think she had ever seen an apple this big in all her life.

Dorothy offered Toto a bite of apple, which he immediately gobbled down. She took a bite of the apple too.

She couldn't possibly eat the huge apple at one time, and it was too heavy to carry for long. So she sliced the rest of it in two and placed one half back into her basket for later. She left the rest of the apple for the forest animals.

That night, for protection from the cold night wind, Toto and Dorothy huddled together in a cave tucked under a nearby cliff. She didn't recall seeing the cliff there earlier. But she and Toto were tired, and Dorothy decided that the cliff was as good as any place to stay for the night.

Dorothy and Toto settled down to sleep. She thought about her basket

and the huge apple for a moment, but she was too tired to care. She and Toto soon fell fast asleep.

Outside, a full moon shined in the Oz sky.

Later, something caused Toto to awake. He stared at the cave entrance for a moment and then started barking.

Startled, Dorothy sat straight up. She thought she saw the shadow of a person walking in the moonlight just outside the cave entrance. With Toto's loud barking, however, whatever it was quickly disappeared from view.

Dorothy and Toto were so exhausted that they soon fell back asleep.

The Cave of the Tinybits

When Dorothy and Toto left the cave the next morning, it seemed even larger than before. Dorothy began to plan another way out of Never Return. She wasn't the type to give up easily.

Just then, she heard Bekama say, "Please come with us."

Startled, Dorothy turned and saw Bekama, who seemed to have appeared out of nowhere. Bekama pointed to another cave entrance nearby. The entrance was barely a foot tall.

That looks more like a hole for a rabbit, Dorothy thought. She asked Bekama, "How can we fit through that small opening?"

"Easy," came the curt reply from Bekama. "You are already shrinking. We only need to accelerate things a bit." Bekama waved her magic wand, and Dorothy and Toto instantly began to shrink faster.

To Dorothy, the trees of the forest became larger, and the cave entrance grew bigger and bigger. Finally she was staring eye to eye at the tiny princess and all the tiny people around her. Now the Tinybits didn't look so small.

"What do you think, Dorothy?" asked Bekama, with a somewhat vicious tone. "Do you think you are small enough to walk through the entrance now?"

Dorothy was speechless. She held Toto tightly in her arms while she stared at the entrance to the cave. She noticed the beautifully detailed cave opening, which was decorated with engravings of gremlins and animals.

At the very top of the entrance, an engraving showed a large kettle with two witches on each side. They held sticks and stirred a witch's brew. The engraving seemed out of place here in the Oz Forest.

Dorothy saw a picture of a lion, a tiger, and a bear. She looked carefully at the picture. The lion there certainly did not look like her friend the Lion. The lion in the picture was a different, most fierce-looking beast. The tiger in the picture looked equally as fierce, and the bear was not as she remembered other bears, the kind of bears who always seemed just fine. The bear in the picture looked very, very mean.

She remembered how the Tin Woodman had warned her about the lions, tigers, and bears that lived in the forest. She remembered his warning from when they first walked down the Yellow Brick Road together.

She couldn't help staring at the ornate cave entrance.

Pulling her thoughts away from the engravings, Dorothy's eyes fell on Bekama's guards. They were dressed just like the Winkie guards she had seen when she was held captive by the Wicked Witch of the West.

Dorothy and Toto followed behind Bekama and the other Tinybits into the cave. Bekama and the others were too busy talking to notice that Dorothy and Toto lagged farther and farther behind.

Dorothy looked back over her shoulder. She could still see the light from the entrance to the cave.

Then an idea occurred to her. She slowed down and quickly moved to one side of the poorly lit cave. She purposely walked slower than Bekama and the others until she could not hear their footsteps.

Then Dorothy took a deep breath, picked up Toto, and with all her nerve, she turned and ran. She held Toto closely to her and ran like she had never run before. The cave entrance loomed in front of them. Soon they were back outside in the sunlight, where Dorothy immediately ran as far away from the cave as she could.

She almost forgot how small she was until she fell over a small mound of dirt about the size of a thimble. Still holding Toto, she stayed where she fell. The cave's entrance was barely in sight.

Dorothy gazed up at the forest around her. The trees seemed so tall, they looked as if they touched the Oz sky. But because she was no taller than tiny, doll-like Bekama, everything around her just seemed larger than ever before.

Dorothy feared that Bekama would soon appear back at the cave's entrance, looking for her and Toto. She thought that something about Bekama was all too familiar, but she decided she could not have met Bekama in the past, because she certainly would have remembered meeting someone only nine inches tall.

While still lying on the ground where she fell, Dorothy noticed Bekama's guards filing out of the cave, heading in her direction. She did not have time to count the number of guards as she stood up and ran with Toto.

The guards called out to her, but by that time Dorothy was far away and could barely hear their shouts. It sounded like they were trying to warn her about something, but she was not in any mood to stop. Too many strange things had happened to her since she and Toto had entered Never Return.

As she ran, Dorothy neared some moss growing at the base of a tree. The moss looked like an ocean of green and gray. She stepped into it and felt it give under her weight. The moss was almost up to her knees, and all you could see of Toto was his head. It was impossible to run through the damp and thick moss.

Dorothy turned to see if Bekama's guards had followed her. Thankfully, she did not see them anywhere, and she could no longer hear their voices. Apparently she had run faster and farther than she thought.

An eerie quiet blanketed the forest as they stood there alone. Dorothy looked around. All the plants seemed huge, the trees gigantic. Because of her size, small rocks now appeared the size of boulders.

There was nothing else to do but begin to walk and see what was up ahead and hope to find a way out.

"If only I could tell Lion, Scarecrow, and Tin Woodman where I am," Dorothy said to Toto. "By now, they must be worried sick. It's long past the time when we were to meet."

Dorothy and Toto split the last piece of apple, which had somehow managed to stay in her basket throughout the day's events. Then Dorothy decided to rest for the night in the soft moss.

However, rain soon rushed down from the Oz sky. The raindrops practically knocked over little Dorothy. Toto couldn't even stand up for long; the rain would knock him down, and just as soon as he struggled back to his paws, another couple of raindrops would hit him, and right back down he would go. He might have drowned had Dorothy not picked him up.

Poor Toto was drenched, and Dorothy was not any better off. The rainwater was pooling on the ground and had already covered the moss where she had planned to rest.

"Quick, Toto!" she exclaimed. "We must find higher ground."

Washed Away

Dorothy spotted a high point of land in the distance and decided to run for it. She took off through the rain, clutching Toto tightly to her chest.

She ran toward the high ground, but as she got closer, she realized she would have to cross a small valley to reach safety. A stream of water flowed in the center of the valley, but it didn't look very deep.

Dorothy started to cross the stream, still holding Toto in her arms. When she was halfway across, she discovered that the water was deeper than she had thought. The current wrapped around her legs, making it hard for her to walk. If she dropped Toto, he certainly would have been carried away.

They were very close to the hill and safety when a tree branch suddenly floated toward her in the fast-moving water. To Dorothy, the tree branch was huge—the leaves looked as big as Auntie Em's blankets.

Dorothy tried to move faster, but she could only struggle slowly against the onrushing current. The huge branch bore down on her. She screamed for help, but her voice was lost in the sound of the churning water.

With one last effort, she lunged toward the high ground to avoid the

branch, but with the force of the water and Toto's extra weight, she missed, and one of the leaves on the branch scooped them up.

The next thing Dorothy knew, she and Toto were on their way, floating down the stream of water on the branch, with the rain continuing to pour down. She and Toto made their way off the leaf and onto the safety of the main branch, where they found a spot under a leaf and sat down. At least the leaf would give them some protection from the heavy rain.

The branch floated its way through the Oz forest. They had a couple of near misses with other floating objects. Then Dorothy noticed a terrible-looking creature at one end of the branch. He apparently was stranded as well.

The creature gazed at her. Toto began to bark. The creature had a pointed head and an oval body covered with black hair. One large spike protruded down from his mouth like a stinger. He used the pincers on the end of his legs to hold on to the branch. His four arms ended in pincers as well.

Dorothy looked into the creature's burning-red eyes and shuddered at the thought that such a hideous thing lived anywhere in Oz. Perhaps there were many more of them, but she hoped not.

It occurred to her that since she was so tiny, she may discover many new creatures that she had not noticed when she was her normal size. The possibility sent a chill down her spine.

Toto finally stopped barking when the portion of the branch that held the creature broke off and veered away from them in the raging water. The creature's red eyes continued to stare at Dorothy until he was out of sight.

Dorothy settled back under her leaf with Toto.

She had little time to rest. The last several hours had been anything but relaxing, and what she saw next was not going to help. Another of those hideous bug-like things was climbing along the branch close by, heading their way. He half crawled and half walked in a slow and determined manner.

Perhaps he is trying hard not to fall into the water, Dorothy surmised.

He slowly moved closer, grasping the branch with his pincers.

Dorothy and Toto had no way to escape. They could retreat to the back of the floating branch, but that would only prolong the confrontation, and it would be dangerous, since the branch continued to lunge and tilt as it rushed downstream.

Eventually, the bug-like creature made its way to where Dorothy and Toto huddled together under the leaf.

"Well, what do I have here?" asked the creature.

"You don't have anything," retorted Dorothy. "But I will introduce myself. I am Dorothy, and this is my dog, Toto. Who are you?"

"It is hard to say," said the creature, who seemed annoyed by the question. "Most people call my kind just plain ole 'bugs.' I hate the reference, but what can I do?"

"But it does not matter what you call me," the bug continued. "What matters is that we are here together on this tree branch, and I am hungry."

Dorothy felt a shiver go up her spine.

"You see, Dorothy, I was sitting on this branch, just about to eat, when the branch broke and fell into the water. Consequently, I missed my meal.

All bugs need to eat and drink, and it appears that you and that Toto animal are the only food on this branch."

The creature's red eyes glared at Dorothy and Toto.

Dorothy held tight to Toto and stood up as best she could. The branch tilted and reeled in the water. All the while she was thinking as fast as she could to try to find a way to escape her tormentor.

"I want you to know," she said as calmly as she could, "I taste terrible, and so does Toto. No one ever eats our kind, because we are so sour."

The bug just laughed. "That really doesn't matter. I can't taste anything, anyway. I don't have any taste buds . . . or taste bugs—sorry, that's just a joke." He chuckled dryly.

Then the creature began to move menacingly closer.

Suddenly, he stopped moving. Bekama and her guards appeared directly in front of him, but they weren't actually there. They looked translucent, like a projected hologram.

Bekama spoke. "Stop! You are not welcome here. You will not injure—nor shall you even touch—Dorothy or Toto. You will crawl back to the end of this branch and stay there until you may safely leave," she commanded. All the while she held her black wand high above her head.

The bug's red eyes opened wide with fear.

Maybe that's where the term "bug-eyed" comes from, Dorothy thought.

The bug turned without a word and half walked, half crawled back to the end of the branch, as ordered by Bekama.

Bekama turned toward Dorothy and Toto. "You were wrong to leave

us back at the cave. I'm sorry I didn't tell you more when we first met, but I was planning on visiting with you safely inside the cave, in my throne room.

"Now you are in quite a fix," Bekama continued. "You see, I cannot help you at this moment, except with advice or by intimidation, as I did when you encountered that Bugaboo."

"Bugaboo? What's a Bugaboo?" asked Dorothy.

"He is a Bugaboo," Bekama pointed to the creature that had threatened to eat Dorothy and Toto. "And he is not a very friendly one. He has a very bad reputation."

"Come to think about it," Dorothy said, "most bugs are not really liked at all. Except ladybugs and butterflies. When I was tall, I would generally not notice bugs, but now that I am so very tiny, I certainly notice them."

Dorothy held on tight as the branch suddenly detoured and headed into the rougher water of a gully. "You must be a good person, Bekama, to want to help Toto and me."

Bekama did not answer. She only smiled a crooked little smile, and her image started to flicker and fade. "I have something to tell you, Dorothy," she said hurriedly. "I have received reports that your friends the Lion, the Scarecrow, and the Tin Woodman are looking for you. They are headed this way."

At first, Dorothy wondered how her three friends could possibly find this place in the middle of the Oz Forest. But then she realized that with the Lion's courage, keen sense of smell, and sharp eyesight, along with

ROGER S. BAUM

the Scarecrow's brain and, of course, all of the Tin Woodman's desire and heart, she already knew the answer to her own question.

Dorothy's thoughts were interrupted as Bekama's image became vivid again. "Dorothy, if your friends enter the land of Never Return, they will become small as well."

Dorothy was taken aback. "Does everyone shrink when they come here?"

Bekama's image began to fade again. "Yes, I'm afraid so. And no one is allowed to leave, because they may come back with evil magic and leave us in ruin. Can you imagine full-sized people coming here and smashing everything in sight? We warn everyone with our signs, yet sometimes the signs are ignored. And then it is too late."

"Is it too late for me?" Dorothy asked with despair in her voice. "All I was doing was taking a shortcut off the Yellow Brick Road."

"Yes, it appears you are here to stay. But my people and I stand ready to help you and Toto as best we can. But we must go for now. We can only maintain our images like this for a short time." Bekama and her guards continued to fade away.

At the last moment, Dorothy called out, "We are hungry."

"Just look for the green-and-red berries. But be careful—do not eat the green-and-purple berries," warned Bekama.

Dorothy yelled out, "Be careful of which berries?"

"Be careful of the green-and. . . ." It was too late, Bekama's voice trailed off into the roar of the water as she and her guards completely disappeared. Dorothy waved good-bye.

THE OZ ODYSSEY

Feeling quite lonely, Dorothy hugged Toto close. She gazed out from under the leaf at the Bugaboo, who was staring into the distance. He remained, as Bekama ordered, at the far end of their floating tree branch.

Bekama must be quite powerful to have this effect on the Bugaboo, Dorothy thought. *And she must be a good person to take the time to help.*

Now she finally had the chance to look around from the floating branch. Because she was so small, even the beautiful flowers along the shore towered above her. She passed many unusual types of flowers and plants as she and Toto floated along.

Suddenly, Dorothy plunged forward. She and Toto were tossed onto dry land as the branch finally struck solid ground. When she sat up, Dorothy could see the Bugaboo racing away as fast as he could. She wondered if this was the last time she would have the misfortune of meeting one of those terrible-looking creatures.

The Lizard of Oz

The rain had stopped. Dorothy stood up and called to Toto, who was busy sniffing the ground. She began to look in earnest for the green-and-red berries Bekama said were safe to eat. Or did she say the green-and-purple berries were safe? Dorothy couldn't remember. All she knew was that she was very hungry, and she assumed that Toto was hungry too.

Luckily, they soon came upon bushes and bushes filled with berries. Some of the berries were green and red, and others were green and purple.

Dorothy looked closely at the berries. They were all about the same size. She smelled a green-and-red berry that hung close to the ground. It smelled a little like a freshly cut apple. Then she smelled a green-and-purple berry. It smelled deliciously the same. Both types of berries smelled good enough to eat. Dorothy had a problem.

She said to Toto, "We can only eat one kind of berry, and I'm not sure which one Bekama said was safe. Oh, and she didn't mention what would happen if we ate the wrong color of berry."

Finally, Dorothy decided she would have to take a chance. She picked out a big, juicy green-and-red berry and closed her eyes to take a bite. But then she opened her eyes and put the green-and-red berry down and instead chose a big, juicy green-and-purple one. She closed her eyes again and opened her mouth to take a bite, but then she stopped.

Dorothy was not sure which kind of berry was safe to eat. She placed the green-and-purple berry down and then picked up the green-and-red berry again and hesitantly bit into it. The berry tasted like an apple. Nothing bad happened. So she took another bite before offering some to Toto.

The green-and-red berry was delicious. Then something wonderful happened. The flavor changed from apple to orange! Dorothy could hardly contain herself. She took another bite, and sure enough, the flavor changed again, this time from orange to banana.

Dorothy placed a green-and-red berry on the ground for Toto. Because he was so small, the berry was too big for him to eat. It would just roll away like a soccer ball when he tried to bite into it.

Toto took a running start and jumped onto the berry. He probably hoped he could smash it into pieces, but the berry merely rolled and Toto was tossed flat on his back.

Dorothy laughed and laughed. She took the berry and tore off a bite for her little friend to eat. Toto took the piece and devoured it. Dorothy wondered what flavor he had gotten; she hoped it was something he liked.

Dorothy considered herself lucky that she had picked the green-and-red berries to eat instead of the green-and-purple ones. She surmised that the green-and-purple berries were the ones Bekama had warned her about.

THE OZ ODYSSEY

With hunger behind them and with the hour late, Dorothy and Toto settled down for the night. She found a berry bush branch, climbed up onto it with Toto, and settled against the trunk of the bush. Both she and Toto were high enough off the ground that Dorothy thought they would be safe for the night.

They slept fitfully. The night was cold, but at least they had each other for warmth.

At dawn they climbed out of the bush and back down to the ground.

As the sun began to dry the land, Dorothy took another green-and-red berry, carefully avoiding the green-and-purple ones. She hoped that the berry would taste like breakfast food. She ended up with chocolate. Not bad, she thought. The taste reminded her of Auntie Em's chocolate milk.

She tried another berry, which turned out to be the flavor of spinach. "Ugh," she cried. She was not particularly fond of spinach, even though she knew that spinach was good for her. Back home in Kansas, Dorothy would sometimes feed Toto a little spinach under the kitchen table when Auntie Em was not watching.

She gave Toto a bite of berry for breakfast. She hoped it tasted good to him. Sure enough, he gobbled it right down.

After a few more bites to fill them up, Dorothy placed some of the smaller berries in her pockets and basket, and she and Toto began to walk again, hoping upon hope to find the way out of this mysterious place.

When you are nine inches tall, everything becomes a challenge to climb over or walk around. The remaining puddles of rainwater from the night before were like large ponds to little Dorothy. When she was her normal size, she would merely walk over them. But now it wasn't so easy.

Fortunately, she and Toto had not met any dangerous animals or other things, not even another Bugaboo. Dorothy wondered if squirrels or rabbits and other animals would also be reduced in size.

She didn't have to wonder long. Just as she came around a log, she saw a lizard with a green, red, and pink body, a large, dark blue head, and a long, forked tongue. The lizard's eyes were as dark as Bekama's, and he was twice as long as Dorothy was tall.

Because he could not see well, the lizard would flick his tongue from time to time, which helped him determine movement by changes in the temperature about him. If the lizard sensed movement near him, it signaled that he might have found a meal for the day.

Suddenly, the lizard turned and faced Dorothy and Toto. His forked tongue flicked the air to locate his meal.

Dorothy instinctively froze. Toto, however, would not stop running about. The large lizard, with his tongue flicking, could sense where Toto was and moved to attack him.

Toto ran and jumped between a small opening in the rocks, but he was not quick enough. The lizard reached for Toto's tail just before he made it into the safety of the rocks. *Clump!* The lizard had Toto's tail firmly between his jaws. Toto barked loudly and squirmed to get loose, but the lizard held firm.

Fortunately, this lizard did not have teeth, but, unfortunately for Toto, he did have strong jaws.

Dorothy forgot about her own safety and ran to Toto. She grabbed his front legs and pulled hard, but Toto could not be budged. The lizard began to shake his head quickly from side to side, trying to pull Toto from Dorothy's grip. If she let go, Toto would surely be swallowed alive.

The lizard raised his head, pulling Dorothy off the ground, but she held on to Toto. The lizard tossed her about faster and faster while his anger grew by the second. Dorothy's shoes flew off her feet, and she could feel the lizard's cold breath on her face. Finally, the lizard stopped for a moment.

While holding on to Toto with one hand, Dorothy quickly grabbed the lizard's tongue with the other and pulled. Then she let go of Toto and grabbed a piece of berry from her dress pocket and threw it down the lizard's throat. Then she grabbed Toto again with both hands.

The berry had the desired effect. The lizard must have thought Toto tasted like the berry. Apparently, the lizard didn't think the berry tasted very good. He opened his jaws wide and threw Toto out.

Toto and Dorothy dropped to the ground with a thud. Then the lizard turned and ran away, completely discouraged.

As Dorothy and Toto watched, a hawk swooped down, clutched the lizard, who made a loud hissing sound, and off they flew. The lizard would soon be a nice meal for the hawk and her babies.

"Now I know another reason why the lizard ran from us." Dorothy smiled. "It serves that lizard right, trying to hurt my Toto."

THE OZ ODYSSEY

Dorothy soon found her shoes, and she and Toto continued on their way.

While she walked, it occurred to Dorothy that she and Toto could have been the hawk's meal, instead of the lizard. It also occurred to her that all the reptiles and certain other creatures were a normal size. It appeared that Bekama and the rest of the people in Never Return were small. Even the Bugaboo was probably normal in size. The lizard and bird were very much normal in size. Dorothy could only wonder why. It was all very confusing.

Dorothy and Toto continued searching. She knew they needed to keep moving to find their way out of this terrible land.

As before, their progress was slow. They were both just too small to step over some rocks, and "little" gullies had now become, for them, dangerously deep. Traveling was very treacherous.

At noon they had lunch from one of the pieces of berry she kept both in her pockets and in her wicker basket.

After a while, Dorothy noticed that the ground had changed to a rusty red. In fact, to her surprise, she and Toto were standing on bricks. Then she realized it was a road.

"A road made of red bricks!" Dorothy said aloud. She remembered that red bricks formed a road near the Yellow Brick Road. Could this be an extension of the Red Brick Road? And if it was, could it lead her and Toto back to safety?

The Sign Maker

Dorothy looked one way down the road and then the other way. She didn't know which direction to travel. If one way ended near the Yellow Brick Road, the other direction could end up anywhere.

Dorothy stood there with Toto, trying to guess which way to go. She decided to go to her left.

Out of nowhere, she heard singing:

> Oh, I'm the Sign Maker,
> I'm the Sign Maker.
> Follow my signs,
> and you will find,
> you're never left behind.
> No, you're never left behind.

Dorothy remembered that the Lion had mentioned meeting the Sign Maker, who had two arms with large hands, two legs, and a large tail on a reptilian body. He carried his road signs, just like the Lion said he had when he met him. Dorothy didn't want anything else to do with reptiles, but the Lion did say that the Sign Maker was a friendly sort of fellow.

When the Sign Maker reached Dorothy, he stopped singing and introduced himself. "Howdy, I'm the Sign Maker. And who might ye be?"

"I'm Dorothy, and this is my dog, Toto."

"Nice to meet you both. May I be of service?"

"Well, maybe you can. First, is this the Red Brick Road people sometimes talk about? You know, the one near the Yellow Brick Road?"

"I would say yes. It's red and it's made of brick, so . . . it is a red-brick road."

"What I mean," said Dorothy, "is this *the* Red Brick Road that leads to the Yellow Brick Road?"

"As the official Sign Maker of Oz, I would say that it is."

"In that case," said Dorothy, "you would know which way leads to the Yellow Brick Road."

The Sign Maker hesitated a moment before answering. "It is that way." He pointed down the Red Brick Road to Dorothy's left.

Since the Sign Maker had come up the road from that direction, she added, "Then you would know for certain, since you just came from that way."

"As certain as the one and only official Sign Maker of Oz can be," he said with a smile.

For some reason, Dorothy was not very comfortable with the Sign Maker's directions, but she decided that since she was absolutely not certain of the correct way to the Yellow Brick Road, she would take his advice and travel the way he suggested.

The Sign Maker reached into his bag of signs and pulled one out. He spun it around a couple of times and stuck it into the ground next to the Red Brick Road. The sign said:

YELLOW BRICK ROAD

THIS WAY

←

"Since I am the official Sign Maker of Oz, this is an official sign giving you the direction to the Yellow Brick Road." He pointed proudly to his newly posted sign.

Dorothy asked, "Since you are heading in the opposite direction, where does the Red Brick Road lead if we follow it the other way?"

The Sign Maker didn't answer. Instead, he said good-bye, and off he went, without further explanation.

Dorothy and Toto turned left and were on their way down the Red Brick Road. As they walked away, they could barely hear the Sign Maker's song fading out in the distance:

Oh, I'm the Sign Maker,

I'm the Sign Maker.

Follow my signs,

and you will find,

you're never left behind. . . .

THE OZ ODYSSEY

Quite some time had passed since Dorothy and Toto parted company with the Sign Maker. They stuck to the Red Brick Road even though it was in disrepair. It was still easier than walking on the bare forest floor.

As they walked along, Dorothy noticed that the Red Brick Road was becoming ever narrower. Now she had more doubts about the Sign Maker's directions, but she figured that since they had come so far in one direction, they might as well stick with it.

The Red Brick Road Village

Toto found a curled leaf with some rainwater cupped in it. Both he and Dorothy took a well-deserved, long, cool drink. She gave Toto another bite from a berry, and she took a bite as well. This time the bite tasted like peach, which delighted her, because she loved peaches. She was never really sure, though, what flavor Toto had gotten.

They took only a moment or two to eat and rest, and then they proceeded down the Red Brick Road. As they moved on, the road meandered and narrowed some more. After rounding a curve, they saw a village in the distance.

Dorothy was ecstatic. Maybe she could find someone there to help them, and maybe she and Toto could have a warm, dry place to sleep for the night, instead of sleeping on the hard ground. Dorothy hadn't slept in a bed for quite some time, and she was sure Toto missed his doggy bed too.

A dirt road detoured off to the right of the Red Brick Road and headed into the village. Dorothy and Toto turned and walked down the road to the village. Dorothy was so excited, she skipped.

THE OZ ODYSSEY

As they neared the village, Dorothy saw a sign in the ground beside the road. The sign read:

RED BRICK ROAD
VILLAGE
POPULATION: 280 201 180
162 148 90 81 76
40 29 18 5 1

Her heart skipped a beat. The village was nearly deserted. The sign indicated that just one person still lived there.

"Come, Toto," Dorothy called. "Population of one or no population, we may have a place to stay for the night. At least I hope so."

As she went through the quiet village, Dorothy noticed that the buildings were well maintained. They had been fashioned for the small people of Never Return and therefore would be just fine for Dorothy and Toto.

The village appeared deserted. The general store was unlit, and the houses were dark. Dorothy continued to be amazed by how well kept the town appeared. The buildings were freshly painted. The road was made of tiny red bricks that were perfectly cut and evenly laid.

Next, Dorothy spotted the town's hotel just ahead. "Perhaps we can spend the night at the hotel," she said to Toto. The hotel's sign was unlit, but she could still read it in the twilight: RED BRICK ROAD VILLAGE HOTEL.

THE OZ ODYSSEY

The hotel appeared to be closed, but the Town Hall next door was ablaze in light. From the street she could hear the laughter and merriment coming from those inside. Lively music mixed with the laughter and conversation. It was quite a party.

Through the windows and the open door, Dorothy could see people dancing. The ladies were dressed in their finest gowns, and the men were formally dressed in tuxedos. Everyone looked exquisitely beautiful and handsome.

Dorothy could see the stage where the band played music with their brightly polished brass instruments. The musicians were dressed in black, and gold braiding adorned their shoulders. The brass buttons on their uniforms gleamed. All together, the musicians reminded her of a military band.

Two guards stood at the doorway. They seemed not to notice Dorothy and Toto, or perhaps they didn't care.

As she and Toto drew closer, Dorothy noticed an elegant chandelier hanging from the center of the ballroom; the fixture emitted most of the light for the grand setting. The hardwood floors were so deeply polished, they mirrored the people dancing.

"Look, Toto, there is Bekama!" Dorothy exclaimed when she saw the only person she knew in Never Return.

She and Toto ran up the steps and into the hall. Dorothy ran over to Bekama. The music and dancing stopped.

"Well, Dorothy, what a surprise," Bekama said. "The last time we

talked, you and your little dog were floating on a tree branch down a river of rainwater. I'm sorry I couldn't be of more help."

"Luckily," Dorothy replied, "we were able to get to dry land and get away from that awful Bugaboo.

"And I still haven't given up," she continued. "I'm still determined to find my way back to the Yellow Brick Road. However, I must admit, it is tough traveling when you are so small."

Everyone in the Town Hall thought what Dorothy said was very funny. They all laughed aloud.

"Oh, I'm sorry," said Dorothy. "I didn't mean to imply that being small was terrible. I just meant that it makes it difficult when you're traveling on foot in the forest."

"We were not laughing at that," said Bekama. "We were laughing because you are trying to find your way back to the Yellow Brick Road. No one leaves Never Return. As a matter of fact, some of us used to be citizens of the Emerald City. We have all tried to leave, but no one has succeeded.

"I must admit, though," Bekama continued, "that it really isn't so bad here in Never Return. We have almost everything one could possibly wish for. We take care of most things ourselves, and the rest is taken care of by some other magical source."

"Magical source?" blurted Dorothy.

"Yes, a magical source," confirmed Bekama. "You probably know her best as the Wicked Witch of the West."

"But I melted her," insisted Dorothy. "I even brought her broomstick back to the Wizard, just as he requested."

"It is true that you melted her, but it is also true that she is still alive. Maybe you only partly melted her, or maybe she had some charm that protected her. Either way, she is alive and well."

"Where is she?" asked Dorothy.

"She lives underground, where the forest rainwater cannot melt her further. She is very busy protecting her Red Brick Road. Consequently, she has devised a way to keep all of us here. Anyone who ignores the warning sign and enters the land of Never Return can never leave.

"Also, from what I understand, because most of her melted away, the Wicked Witch of the West is now tiny. That is why she makes everyone in Never Return tiny as well, because she is very angry that she is so small."

Dorothy thought a moment. "What about the Sign Maker?" she asked. "And you have magic, Bekama."

"That's true, but I have only what little magic the Wicked Witch allows me," explained Bekama. "As far as the Sign Maker is concerned, he comes and goes as he wishes. We don't understand how he does it. He seems to be a nice creature, but he is obviously a friend of the Wicked Witch."

Bekama turned and ordered the band to play again. It wasn't long before everyone was back to their merriment. Dorothy had become just another guest at Bekama's dance.

Just as Bekama was about to talk with another guest, Dorothy interrupted and said, "Bekama, would you answer a question? When you enter the village, there is a sign that says only one person lives here, and yet the dance hall is filled with all these guests."

Bekama turned away from her guest to answer Dorothy. "Those of us who have moved away from the village come here once a year, to help relive the memories of the good old days when this town was a thriving place and the buildings and the people who lived here were normal size, instead of just inches tall," said Bekama dryly.

"At least the dance hall is thriving," observed Dorothy. "And look, everyone is eating the green-and-red berries."

"Yes, aren't they fun? You never know what flavor will come next. I see that you took my advice and avoided the green-and-purple berries."

"Oh, yes, I took your advice," said Dorothy. "I only eat the green-and-red ones. I really wasn't sure which colors were correct—the first time, I almost ate a green-and-purple one!"

Bekama quickly changed the subject. "I'm sorry to disappoint you, Dorothy. I realize that you just arrived, but the party is almost over, and people will be leaving soon."

Dorothy felt let down for a moment, as she had hoped to enjoy the party, and then she asked, "Bekama, would it be okay if Toto and I stayed at the hotel for the night?"

"I don't see why not," answered Bekama with a smile plastered across her face. "I haven't seen the Wicked Witch for some time, so I suppose you could stay here without her knowing it. Indeed, she may not be aware that you are here in Never Return. If she did know, I'm not sure what she would do. Especially since you almost succeeded in destroying her."

Dorothy was taken aback by Bekama's remark.

"By the way," Bekama continued, "to answer your question, this village does have a population of just one. Let me introduce you to him."

Bekama touched a nearby guest on the arm. The guest turned and smiled broadly.

"Mr. Mayor," said Bekama, "I would like you to meet Dorothy and her little dog, Toto."

"How do you do, Dorothy," said the cheery mayor, who was dressed in his finest attire.

"How do you do," replied Dorothy.

"What do we have here?" The mayor reached down and patted Toto on the top of his furry head.

"This is my dog, Toto," answered Dorothy.

"He is a nice dog," replied the mayor.

"Thank you," said Dorothy. "It is nice to meet the mayor of Red Brick Road Village. I understand that you are the only person living here."

"That is true," said the mayor, "though I am merely a self-appointed mayor, since I'm the only one living here."

"Where is everyone else?" asked Dorothy.

Before the mayor could answer, Bekama interrupted and raised her voice above the others. "It looks like it is going to rain. I'm afraid it's time

to leave until our next Town Hall Ball."

The orchestra stopped playing, and everybody and everything stood frozen in time for just a moment.

Bekama turned quickly, grinned at Dorothy, and said, "Until I see you again, my dear."

In a flash, the dance hall was empty of all guests except Dorothy, Toto, and the mayor.

The mayor said, "I guess your question about Red Brick Road Village and its population has been answered. I'm the only resident left here in the Town Hall, and in all the rest of the village, for that matter."

"But why are you the only one left in the village?" asked Dorothy.

"To tell you the truth, I'm really not quite sure where everyone has gone—they just disappeared one at a time over the years. I never quite understood why.

"Now I really must beg your leave," he continued. "I understand that you are staying at our hotel. I hope you find the accommodations satis-factory—you need your sleep, and I bet Toto is tired too. Please make yourself at home. I'm sure I'll see you in the morning."

The mayor gave his farewell. "Good night, Dorothy, and good night to you, Toto. At least for a while, we can say that the village has a population of three." He chuckled and then walked out the door.

"Good night, Mr. Mayor," Dorothy yelled after him. "And thank you."

Suddenly, she felt very alone standing in the middle of the deserted Town

Hall where, just minutes earlier, laughter and music had filled the room. She picked up Toto, gave him a quick hug, and carried him out the front door into the moonlight. Then she walked down the deserted street to the empty hotel.

The Red Brick Road Village Hotel

The hotel lobby was dark and very quiet. A window shutter swung lazily in the evening breeze, tapping one of the partially open windows. Dorothy heard no other sounds.

The moonlight filtering through the windows allowed her to see the room. She found a candle holder and a candle near the hotel's registration desk, so she began to look for matches. As soon as she started to look, the candle lit on its own. Dorothy was so startled, she almost dropped it.

Holding the candle in one hand, she placed Toto down on the floor and walked over to the antique oak registration desk. The hotel's guest book was open. Dorothy looked down the pages at the names of former guests. She could not help but notice the last entry in the book. Her eyes opened wide in surprise. The last guest listed was "Dorothy Gale," with a note beside the name, "and her dog, Toto—Room 3-21."

By now, she was very tired. Dorothy just didn't have the energy to think about the village or the hotel and the other peculiar things that had happened.

She took the candle and carefully walked up the old staircase to find room number 3-21. She assumed that she needed to find room 21 on the third floor. As she walked, the stairs creaked and groaned with every step. Dorothy's hands tightened around the candle holder. As she and Toto ascended toward the landing, the flickering candlelight caused their shadows to dance between the stairs, the railings, and the walls.

More than once, strange shadows of people and creatures danced beside Dorothy's and Toto's own shadows. The shadow of a wicked witch upon her broom flew by.

Toto stayed close to Dorothy. As they reached the top of the stairs, he barked loudly.

Dorothy nearly fell when Toto barked, but she managed to grab the handrail with one hand and hold on to the candle with the other. She didn't know what had frightened little Toto.

Finally, they made it to the third floor. Dorothy held the candle high to see the room numbers. She walked down the hall until the candlelight shined on the door to room 3-21.

The key to the room was in the keyhole below the doorknob. Dorothy turned the key, removed it, and then turned the doorknob. The door easily and quietly swung open.

Toto ran into the room ahead of her.

Inside, the room was neat and clean, which surprised Dorothy, especially considering that no one was around to care for the hotel. Perhaps the room had seen no other guests for a long time, though she did not

notice much dust. The deep brown of the polished, old wood furniture glowed in the candlelight.

The room contained a chair, a dresser, a bed, and a closet. Another door opened to a small bathroom.

Dorothy closed the front door and locked it. She placed the key on the dresser along with the candle holder. She then walked over to the room's only window. She drew back the curtains and courageously peeked out.

It appeared the third floor was also the top floor of the hotel. Dorothy could barely see a thing in the darkness outside, but she had a strange feeling that she was peering down into the barnyard at Uncle Henry and Auntie Em's house. She could almost see the chicken coop and barn and the corral attached to the barn. My eyes must be playing tricks on me, she thought.

She closed the curtain and turned from the window just as Toto jumped up onto the bed. "That's a good idea," said Dorothy. "It's way past bedtime. I'm going to bed too."

As an afterthought, she opened a dresser drawer and was surprised to find a full set of clothes, as well as items such as a hair brush and comb. She even found another gingham dress and some hair ribbons.

By now, Dorothy was so tired, she didn't have any further thoughts except to sleep. She washed and quickly crawled into bed, and very soon she and Toto were fast asleep.

That night, Dorothy dreamed of Auntie Em, Uncle Henry, and the farm. In her dream, it was early morning. Toto was with her, and she had just finished milking the cows when she heard Auntie Em ringing the old bell that hung just outside the back door at the farmhouse. It was time for breakfast. She ran from the barn and into the farmhouse.

When Dorothy rushed through the door, Auntie Em announced, "Breakfast is ready and hot, so hurry and wash your hands and sit down before it gets cold."

Uncle Henry was already sitting at the table. The rest of Dorothy's farmhouse friends had already eaten their fill and had left to tend to the animals and fields.

Dorothy quickly returned after washing and sat down at the breakfast table in her usual place. "Good morning, Uncle Henry," she said, smiling brightly.

"Good morning," Uncle Henry answered in his normal, matter-of-fact voice.

Dorothy almost laughed out loud. Uncle Henry had just put down a glass of milk, and he had a big, white milk mustache across the top of his lip.

"Here, Uncle Henry, use this napkin and wipe your lip. You look like you have a mustache." Dorothy giggled.

Auntie Em placed a plate of fresh eggs and bacon and a bowl of oatmeal in front of her. "Make sure you eat it all, Dorothy," she said.

In her dream, Dorothy took a spoon from the table and looked at the food. The bowl of oatmeal was so tiny, it was almost the size of a thimble. The plate of bacon and eggs was barely an inch across.

"Stop staring at your food and eat, Dorothy," scolded Auntie Em. "How are you going to grow up and stay healthy unless you eat?"

THE OZ ODYSSEY

Dorothy looked at Auntie Em and started to say something, when she suddenly woke up with a start. She sat straight up in the hotel-room bed. Toto was still asleep next to her on his back, with all four of his paws up in the air. *I wish I could sleep as soundly as Toto,* she thought.

The morning sun was peeking through the curtains. Dorothy had the strangest feeling about the night, not only because of her dream but also because of what she thought she saw outside her hotel window. She walked over and opened the curtains wide to let in the sunshine. When she looked outside, all she saw were the deserted streets and empty buildings of the village.

Dorothy remembered the fresh clothes in the dresser and decided that if everything fit, she would change. First she bathed Toto and dried him off with one of the convenient bath towels. Then she took a warm bath. The bath felt good, after such a long time without one.

Finally, she dressed. The clothes in the dresser drawer fit perfectly. Then she left the hotel room.

Dorothy and Toto went downstairs to the lobby. The candles had been extinguished, and the lobby was just as deserted as the night before. However, a plate of bacon and eggs and a bowl of oatmeal sat on the lobby table.

The meal was just like the one in her dream, only now the plate and bowl did not look tiny. They were normal size—or were they? Dorothy realized that the meal was just as small as it had been in her dream. It looked normal size now because she and Toto were so tiny themselves.

"Oh, well, I might as well eat while I have the chance," Dorothy said to Toto. It was the first real meal that she'd had in days. She shared it with Toto.

"I wonder who prepared this food?" she asked. "Here, Toto, here is a bite of bacon for you."

He eagerly swallowed the bacon whole.

Dorothy finished her breakfast in the quaint and quiet old hotel. She looked around one last time before going outside. She took a few steps toward the front door and then stopped a moment to look back at the table in the lobby. The dirty plates had disappeared, and the table was as clean as it had been when she first entered the hotel.

Dorothy, with Toto close behind, decided to go back inside and look at the hotel guest book. Her name was still written there as before, but she noticed that someone had checked her out at exactly 11:00 A.M. She looked around but did not see anybody. The wall clock read 11:59 A.M. She quickly grabbed her basket and walked out into the sunlight.

Leaving the Red Brick Road Village

Dorothy and Toto walked to the Red Brick Road. "Let's go, Toto," she said. "We have to find our way out of this land. Can you imagine how worried our friends must be?"

The clock in the village's bell tower began to chime the hour. One, two. . . .

Just then, the mayor came running up to Dorothy and Toto. He was out of breath.

The bell continued its count. Five, six. . . .

The mayor quickly tipped his hat and said, "Thank you for visiting my village. I hope you will come again someday."

Eight, nine. . . .

"Thank you for your hospitality, Mr. Mayor. I would certainly like to visit again and see more of your wonderful village. Perhaps—" Dorothy started to say something, but the clock's bell interrupted her.

Ten, eleven . . . the remaining seconds ticked off before high noon.

Dorothy was about to finish her sentence, but as the clock chimed noon, she looked at the mayor, and for a split second he looked like the Wicked Witch of the West. Then the mayor and the village vanished right before her eyes.

The welcome sign for the Red Brick Road Village still stood. Dorothy went to look at it, and to her amazement, the population had been reduced by one and now stood at zero.

She noticed that she and Toto, at the moment the town disappeared, had been standing on the Red Brick Road, just one step outside of the town's border. Perhaps this had saved them from vanishing along with the mayor. The mayor had been standing just within the town's borders, and he had disappeared.

Had she lingered in the hotel any longer, she and Toto would still have been inside the village at the stroke of noon and probably would have vanished. Perhaps that was why the breakfast had been prepared for her, to stall her in the hotel.

Dorothy wondered what it all meant. She should have never, ever left the Yellow Brick Road.

"Now I am nine inches tall," she said, "lost somewhere in the Oz Forest, in a land called Never Return. What can I do?"

Dorothy hesitated a moment and then decided to travel down the Red Brick Road in the same direction as before.

She noticed that a river ran alongside this section of the road, and on the opposite side, huge thorn bushes grew thick. As they rounded a curve, the road dipped below the water's surface.

Dorothy and Toto stopped at the water's edge. It appeared that they could go no farther. Water filled the horizon as far as their eyes could see, except for the forbidding thornbushes, though even they eventually dipped below the water.

I guess we'll have to go back the way we came, Dorothy reasoned. Completely discouraged, she was about to turn around and head back down the Red Brick Road, when she noticed a small boat heading their way.

Eventually, the boat stopped near them at the water's edge. To Dorothy's amazement, no one manned the craft. It was if the boat was just waiting for her and Toto.

She looked around. The boat didn't seem unusual, except that it was small enough to fit the little people of Never Return. Finally, Dorothy decided she and Toto would use the boat to continue in the same direction. The Red Brick Road could be seen below the clear water, so she could follow it in the boat. If she lost sight of the road, she could always go back. She was a little upset at the Sign Maker, because he didn't mention any obstacles such as this one.

Dorothy lifted Toto into the rowboat and then climbed in herself. She reached for the oars, but to her surprise, the boat pulled away from the shore under its own power.

She noticed the words "Tugg Jr." on the side of the boat. The boat seemed to have a mind of its own, or perhaps someone or something was controlling it, because it moved in a purposeful direction.

To Dorothy's consternation, Tugg Jr. moved away from the sunken Red

Brick Road. Dorothy tried to turn the boat with the oars, but she could not. The oars just helped to splash water on her and Toto. She looked behind her, and what she could see of the Red Brick Road became smaller and smaller as they moved farther and farther away. Soon, she could not see anything around them except water.

Thank goodness they were floating on fresh water, so she could have a drink to quench her thirst. She cupped her hands and scooped up some water so Toto could drink as well. There was nothing Dorothy could do but wait and see where Tugg Jr. was taking them.

She and Toto cuddled up at nightfall and gazed into the starlit night. The moon was full, and she thought she saw the silhouette of the Wicked Witch cross in front of it.

Needless to say, Dorothy had trouble falling asleep.

An Old Mansion

Dorothy was awakened by the voice of Bekama. "It will not be long now. It will not be long now," the raspy voice repeated in the cool night air.

The words puzzled Dorothy, and she wondered what they meant. She was too tired to think about it for long, however, and she was soon back asleep.

When she and Toto woke up, the sun was shining through the mist of the early morning.

"Hello, Dorothy. Hello to you, Toto."

Dorothy looked over the side of the rowboat, and there stood Bekama on the Red Brick Road. She vanished from sight before Dorothy could greet her in return, leaving Dorothy puzzled.

Once she was fully awake, Dorothy looked around. Sometime during the night, Tugg Jr. had carried them to the shore, right at the Red Brick Road. The little boat drifted to land, and Dorothy and Toto got out without even getting their feet wet.

They walked down the Red Brick Road in the bright morning sunshine. As they rounded a curve, the Red Brick Road began to climb. After rounding another curve, Dorothy saw an old mansion ahead at the top of the hill.

The old mansion was very dark. It was constructed of huge gray stones that had aged with time. Dorothy and Toto went up the short walk to the heavy wooden front doors that had large iron hinges.

At the door, all Dorothy could hear was Toto's panting and the rustling leaves on the vines crawling up the outside walls of the mansion. The vines used every crack and crevice to anchor themselves to the old gray stones. An occasional puff of wind would cause the leaves to rustle, adding to the creepiness of the place.

As they stood before the heavy doors, Dorothy thought about avoiding the place altogether, but she wondered if the mansion might hold a clue about how to get out of Never Return. She took a deep breath and knocked. The door was so thick, her knock made only a dull thud. She didn't see a doorbell or knocker to help.

Dorothy set her basket down, removed one of her shoes, and hit the door with its heel. The shoe made a little more noise, but it still wasn't loud enough for anyone to hear, unless they were standing very close to the door.

She put her shoe back on and kicked the door hard. "Ouch!" she yelled. Her kick caused the door to open slightly. It was unlocked! Dorothy leaned against the heavy door and opened it more, the rusty hinges squeaking loudly.

THE OZ ODYSSEY

The sunlight pierced the dark entryway. Toto scampered inside ahead of Dorothy.

"Stop, Toto, stop!" she yelled. "Stay close to me."

But Toto didn't obey her, and he was soon out of sight, gone somewhere inside the dark mansion. She could still hear him bark, but the sound faded as he ran farther away. She called him again, but Toto did not return. It was unusual for Toto not to obey her.

The dark mansion gave her the creeps, and now Toto was lost somewhere inside.

"Toto, come," Dorothy commanded. To her relief, she heard him bark again, but he sounded miles and miles away. She had no choice but to go in and find him.

The farther she moved from the doorway and the sunlight outside, the darker it became. Indeed, Auntie Em, Uncle Henry, and all of her Oz friends seemed farther away then ever.

"Poor Lion, Scarecrow, and Tin Woodman," Dorothy said to no one in particular. "They must be completely worried sick." And now, on top of everything else, she was worried sick about Toto.

Every so often at hallway intersections, a narrow beam of light would shine down from small mirrors in the ceiling. The mirrors were positioned to reflect the sunlight outside into the dark interior of the mansion.

She noticed that the hall floor was made from the same red brick as the Red Brick Road. Was it possible that the Red Brick Road ran through the mansion?

Soon the hallways became a maze. Dorothy was helplessly lost. She felt she would never find Toto or a way out of the mansion.

The red-brick hallway eventually sloped downward. Dorothy passed several doors. Hoping she might see Toto, she finally opened one. The room was a library, with row upon row of shelves lined with old books.

Several candle lamps illuminated the room, which contained several soft-cushioned reading chairs. Dorothy walked to a row of shelves labeled "History." She began to read the titles, which included *The United States of America, The Autobiography of George Washington, Benjiman Franklin, George Washington Carver, The Lewis and Clark Expedition, The Civil War, Pearl Harbor,* and *The History and Battles of World War I and World War II.*

Some of the books were about places and people Auntie Em and Uncle Henry had told her about. Some were not even in her school library any longer. She wondered why. *History is history,* she told herself.

One title on another shelf, *The Complete Works of Edgar Allen Poe,* caught Dorothy's attention. Auntie Em had told her about Edgar Allen Poe. She pulled the beautiful, leather-bound book off the shelf. She opened the heavy cover and turned to the first page, which showed the title and the author's name. She turned to the next page, only to find it blank. She turned to the next page, and it too was blank. She flipped through the rest of the book and discovered that all of the pages were blank. It was as if the print had been removed.

Dorothy quickly grabbed a couple more of the old books. She opened

THE OZ ODYSSEY

Gulliver's Travels. Its pages were blank. She opened *The Red Badge of Courage*—blank again.

Why, all these books have blank pages, she thought. *All this history and knowledge is gone.*

She heard Toto's faint bark and turned to leave the room. As she started to walk out the door, a fire flared nearby. Dorothy turned to see an old man rise from a chair by the glowing fireplace. She had not noticed anyone in the room when she came in. The old man turned toward her, setting the book in his hand on a small table by the chair.

The book was titled *All the World's Knowledge*.

"Welcome to my library," said the nice-looking gentleman, smiling.

"Hello," said Dorothy.

"I'm glad you could visit, Dorothy," he replied.

She was startled. "How do you know my name?"

"I read, so I learn things. Special things. Indeed, you might say I met you quite some time ago, in a book called *The Wonderful Wizard of Oz,* and in other Oz books as well."

"A book?" asked Dorothy.

"Yes, many books. You have had some wonderful adventures."

"Why, thank you, sir," she said, somewhat flabbergasted. "I am sorry, but I really must hurry off. My dog, Toto, ran away from me. He is somewhere in this mansion, and I am really must find him."

"Yes, I know," said the tall man.

"By the way, what is your name?" asked Dorothy.

"Officially, I am called the Royal Historian of Oz. But you may call me Frank, particularly since I already know you so well."

"Good-bye, Frank. By the way," Dorothy said as she reached the door, "why are all the pages of these beautiful books blank?"

The Royal Historian smiled. "You see," he said, "many have been condensed or have been eliminated from literature. So I keep them alive by at least their covers. However, it is a shame that the words are gone, isn't it?"

"Yes, it is," she agreed. "Thank you for remembering me." She closed the door behind her as Frank began to sit back down by the fireplace. Dorothy had a funny feeling she had met him before.

Books with me in them! she thought. *I'll have to read those someday.* Her thoughts were interrupted by Toto's barking. She ran down the hall to find him. For a moment she wondered how the Royal Historian knew about Toto and the fact that he was lost.

The Girl
of the Clouds

Dorothy ran farther down the sloping red-brick hallway until she found herself in front of a large pool of water. The pool was lit by a beam of light that poured down from the ceiling. The room was large, and the ceiling was very, very tall.

The walls of the oval room were painted with pictures of witches and goblins, of water and fire, and of dragons. One section was a mural of stars, including a green star, against the black of night.

Then something else caught Dorothy's eye—a painting that looked like a map, with a Red Brick Road running through it! She followed the road with her eyes. It started near Munchkin Land and traveled in the direction of the old castle of the Wicked Witch of the West. Dorothy saw many things that were familiar to her, but many others were not.

Dorothy could see a door on the other side of the pool, and she wondered if she should wade across to the other side. When she heard Toto's bark come from the direction of the door, she knew she had no other choice.

THE OZ ODYSSEY

Dorothy took off her shoes and held them high above her head. As she was about to jump into the pool, the light from the ceiling vanished. Only the stars in the mural, glowing silver, emitted light. The water in the pool reflected the light of the sparkling silver stars.

Then Dorothy heard a slight gurgling sound, and she took a step backward. As she watched, the water quickly drained from the pool, exposing a large crystal globe on a white-marble pedestal sitting in the center of the pool.

The globe radiated a pure silver light. Its light, along with the silver light from the stars on the mural, gave the room an eerie glow.

Dorothy carefully walked down the steps leading to the bottom of the pool. She walked over to the globe and reached out to touch its smooth surface. As soon as she touched it, the silver light changed to emerald green. The globe rose into the air above the pedestal and hovered there.

A young girl's voice came from within the globe. "Only one person in Oz has the power to empty the pool and reveal me."

"Who are you?" asked Dorothy.

"I am Micur, the Girl of the Clouds."

"Why are you inside the globe?" Dorothy asked.

"I was put here for disobeying Bekama."

"But I thought Bekama was a good person," said Dorothy, perplexed.

"She is always nice, at first, until you disobey her, and then she will do anything she wants to you. She is the most evil witch—you know her as the Wicked Witch of the West, and you know that her evil magic is very powerful.

"One day, she distracted me at my home in the sky and placed me in this globe. You see, Dorothy, my magic is very powerful too, but my magic is good magic. I follow the example of your friend Glinda, the Good Witch of the South. She is my personal example of goodness. I look up to her."

"I'm sorry you fell under Bekama's spell. But why are you over this pedestal in the center of this pool?" asked Dorothy.

"Bekama put me in this globe, but I made the pool. The water protects me from further harm from Bekama—you know how she hates water."

"I certainly do," said Dorothy. "Isn't it lonely in that globe here in the center of this pool?" she asked.

"Yes," answered Micur. "But I have many friends, and I created the magic mural to help me feel at home."

"You did the mural? It is beautiful."

"Thank you," answered Micur. "I painted it with my imagination and my dreams."

"Well, it is indeed beautiful," Dorothy commented again. "So, by the look of things, you must be filled with lots and lots of imagination and dreams."

"It is the way of our clan, of good mystics, of good philosophers, and of thoughtful teachers."

"Where do you normally live?" asked Dorothy.

"I live in the sky, where dreams are made and where imagination strikes like lightning with the roar of thunder. When you hear thunder and see lightning, it very often means that someone's dreams and imagination have created something really very special."

"How wonderful!" said Dorothy. "What is the name of your home in the sky above Oz?"

"Well, Dorothy, my homeplace is not just over Oz, it is over the whole world. Our home is called Wingsong. Most of the time my people are invisible, but every once in a while you can see us in the clouds."

"I think I have seen you in the clouds," said Dorothy, smiling. "Why, I have seen animals and fish and people. As a matter of fact, I have seen lots of things in the clouds. Why, just the other day I even saw a large cloud that looked like the face of my Auntie Em."

"It appears you use your imagination as well, Dorothy," said Micur with a smile within her voice.

Then Dorothy became perplexed. "So, Bekama is really the Wicked Witch of the West in disguise?"

"Yes. She hides here in these deep Oz woods, capturing anyone who trespasses in her territory of Never Return. She cast a spell on the Sign Maker, who normally is harmless, to get him to send people here to be captured."

"That's what happened to me," said Dorothy, who recalled her conversation with the funny-looking Sign Maker. "Why is she doing all this mischief?" she asked.

"She is biding her time until she can gather her full strength and capture the Emerald City, as well as Glinda or anyone else that gets in her way. She will use the people here to help her accomplish her goal of dominating Oz. She is building a new Winkie army. Of course, many of these people are good, but they are under her evil spell."

"How come she is letting me remain free?" asked Dorothy.

"I'm sure she is just toying with you while she waits for your friends to show up—that is, if they make it this far safely."

"Oh, no! You mean my friends Lion, Scarecrow, and Tin Woodman are still looking for us?"

"Yes," said Micur. "It is slow going in this forest, as you know, because of all the different creatures that live here, not to mention the thick woods."

"How do you know all about them, when you are here in this globe?" asked Dorothy, hoping Micur could somehow help them with her magic.

Micur thoughtfully answered, "I know of them because I can feel their presence within you, Dorothy. It is my nature."

"Is Toto okay? Is he safe?"

"He is waiting patiently for you at the door on the other side of this empty pool."

"Thank you. Oh, thank you," said Dorothy. She was relieved and very grateful for the information.

"You must go now," warned Micur. "The witch will soon find you."

Dorothy quickly asked, "How can I return to my normal size?"

"I understand there is only one way, and Bekama keeps it a well-guarded secret. You must find the answer yourself. If I tell you, the spell will become permanent. Just please remember the berries. That is all I can say."

THE OZ ODYSSEY

When Micur finished speaking, water began to refill the pool. The crystal globe, with Micur inside, began to descend back down to the top of the pedestal.

Dorothy ran to the stairs opposite where she entered the pool. When she reached the foot of the stairs, the water began to pour into the pool faster. She ran up the stairs, the water rising at her heels with each step. She stopped at the top of the stairs and turned to look back at the globe. The water had covered the top of the pedestal and soon would cover the globe as well.

Before she left, she said, "Good-bye, Micur, and with good luck perhaps we will meet again someday."

"I hope so, Dorothy," said Micur excitedly. "I'm glad you came here— you have given me more ideas for my mural. Good-bye, Dorothy, and please remember. . . ." She paused—the water had almost covered the globe. "Please remember the berries. . . ." Her words trailed off as the water covered the globe.

"Please remember the berries," Dorothy repeated. Then she looked at the mural. A beautiful new painting of her and Toto on the Yellow Brick Road had been added to Micur's fantastic work. She thought it was a good omen to see herself together with Toto, but still she wondered what it all meant.

Dorothy looked around. Along with the glowing stars on the mural, the silver light from the sunken globe illuminated the room.

Dorothy and Toto Reunite

Dorothy walked to the door by the pool and opened it. Suddenly, she felt a furry little body jump up into her arms, nearly knocking her backward into the pool.

"Toto!" she cried. "Toto, you've come back. Never run away from me again," she gently scolded, half laughing and half crying.

She turned around and looked back at the pool. She could see the globe's silver glow dim and finally disappear. Then the light from the ceiling again beamed into the room, lighting it completely.

It was difficult for Dorothy to believe that tiny Bekama was really the Wicked Witch of the West, but Micur certainly seemed to know what she was talking about.

Dorothy was very worried about her friends, because they had placed themselves in harm's way all because she had made the stupid mistake of traveling off the Yellow Brick Road.

With Toto safely under one arm, she walked through the door and into another hallway. The old mansion seemed to be filled with room after room, all connected by hallways filled with spider webs. She walked down the hall, trying her best to avoid the sticky, dusty webs.

Dorothy turned to her right every time she came to a corner, hoping she would eventually make a complete trip around the mansion and return to the front door. Except for meeting Frank and Micur, she wished she had never entered this old place.

She stopped a moment and reached into her pocket for a piece of berry. She gave Toto a bite and then took a bite herself. This time, the berry tasted like a delicious orange. The flavor reminded her of the fresh oranges her Auntie Em would buy in town back in Kansas.

While she ate, Dorothy puzzled over Micur's mysterious statement about the berries.

After they finished their snack, Toto and Dorothy slowly made their way through the creepy, musty, old mansion. Apparently, no one had traveled down the halls for a long, long time.

After more than an hour, Dorothy and Toto found themselves back at the front door. She almost wanted to stay just a moment longer and open a few more of the doors to fulfill her curiosity about what might be behind them. But her common sense told her to leave.

With Toto under her arm, Dorothy pulled hard on the front door and managed to open it. She walked into the sunlight, finding her basket right where she had left it. Then she closed the door of the old mansion behind her. The door gave a moaning squeak, as if it were trying to indicate its displeasure with the fact that Dorothy and Toto had found their way out.

She placed Toto on the ground and walked around to the back of the mansion. Sure enough, the Red Brick Road did travel through the mansion and back out the other end. She could only wonder why.

Dorothy glanced up to the roof of the mansion, where she saw a statue of the Mayor of Munchkin Land. The statue perplexed her. Why was a statue of the Mayor of Munchkin Land on top of this old mansion in Never Return?

She didn't have time to think about this odd situation very long. She headed with Toto down the Red Brick Road, hoping upon hope that it would lead her to the Yellow Brick Road. Indeed, the statue of the Mayor of Munchkin Land was somewhat encouraging. Someday, she would have to find out why it was atop the mansion.

After traveling a while, Dorothy and Toto reached a silver bridge. They saw a land of flowers and beauty on the other side, so they began to cross the bridge.

Suddenly, Bekama appeared in the middle of the bridge, blocking their way. "I'm sorry, Dorothy," she said, "you cannot travel any farther. On the other side of this bridge is the home of the Flower of Oz—the Lion probably told you all about her. As you must know, she represents all that is good in Oz. I cannot let you pass."

"Well," said Dorothy, "the Lion did tell me about the Flower of Oz and all her goodness, and someone else just recently told me all about you."

"All about me? What do you mean, all about poor little me?"

"The person told me how wicked you are. She told me you are the Wicked

Witch of the West. I thought I had destroyed you, but I guess I didn't. If I had known it, I would have finished you then."

"Maybe you would have, but you're too late now." The tiny Wicked Witch smiled defiantly.

"Now I understand," Dorothy replied, "why you appeared as an image while I was floating on that branch in the river and all the while it was raining. You couldn't allow the water to touch you. And now I also realize why all your guards remind me of the ones I saw in your castle."

"I never realized," replied the Wicked Witch, "that you and that nasty little dog of yours had any brains at all, but apparently you do."

"Yes, I do, and I'm smart enough to know that you are merely waiting for Lion, Scarecrow, and Tin Woodman to arrive, and then you plan to invade the Emerald City."

The Wicked Witch scowled. "Only a couple of people could guess my plan. You have been talking with Micur, and she told you these things. There should only be one ruler of Oz, located in the Emerald City, and, of course, that will be me." She cackled loudly.

Now Dorothy and Toto were in more danger than ever before. She now knew that Bekama, who she thought was helping her out of kindness, was really the Wicked Witch of the West, her old enemy. Dorothy frantically tried to think of a way to get around the Wicked Witch and across the Silver Bridge. *If only my friends were here to help me,* she thought.

PART II

THE SEARCH BEGINS

Dorothy's Friends
Find Her Trail

"We must find them," said the Tin Woodman.

"And the sooner, the better," added the Scarecrow.

"I'm doing the best I can," said the Lion, his nose sniffing the ground for Dorothy's scent as the group moved into the dark forest.

If Dorothy hadn't accidentally dropped an apple core on the side of the Yellow Brick Road, her friends would not have had a clue as to her where-abouts. The apple core was a way off the road; the Lion spotted it with his keen eyesight. He frantically searched for Dorothy's scent, which he soon found at the edge of the Oz Forest, not far from the Yellow Brick Road.

Though night had fallen, the friends decided to continue. They feared that Dorothy could be in trouble, and time was of the essence.

The Tin Woodman used his knowledge of the woods to construct a torch out of wood and some tall dry grass. After several tries, he lit the torch with a spark he made by striking his ax against a piece of flint.

The three friends—the Lion, the Scarecrow, and the Tin Woodman—stayed close together. The Scarecrow, however, stayed as far away from the Tin Woodman's torch as he could. As everyone knows, fire and straw just don't mix well.

With the Lion leading the way, they followed Dorothy and Toto's scent deeper into the forest. In the darkness of night, the trees and plants appeared sinister. The torchlight caused their shadows to dance.

Eerie sounds filled the dark forest. The dancing shadows together with the weird noises caused the Lion to stop for a moment. He looked about and said, "I'm glad I'm not a coward any longer, or I would turn around and run."

The thick forest slowed their progress, and although the Tin Woodman and the Scarecrow didn't tire, the Lion did. Nonetheless, he trudged onward, fearing for Dorothy's well-being.

An owl called above the rest of the forest noise. "Who-who-whooooo, who-who-whooooo."

"It's me, it's me," the Scarecrow answered jokingly.

By now, their torch had nearly burned out. The Tin Woodman hastily made a new one and lit it from the dying flames of the first. They made sure that the used torch was completely out by covering it with dirt, and then the three rescuers were on their way again.

The Lion continued to lead the way as he tried to stay on Dorothy and Toto's trail. As they moved along, they entered a peculiar part of the forest where the colors were very bright. The leaves on the trees were exceptionally bright green, and they shimmered in the moonlight. The torch illuminated many beautiful flowers growing around them.

The three friends slowly made their way, ducking under branches and stepping over fallen trees. Then they came to an area covered with terrible thornbushes. The thorns ripped and tore at anything that brushed by the bushes.

The Tin Woodman hoisted the Lion up onto his shoulders so the thorns could not hurt him. The Tin Woodman was not hurt by thorns because, after all, he was made of metal.

The Tin Woodman made small talk to help keep his mind off their serious situation. "Indeed," he said, "there are some advantages when your body is made of metal. These thorns don't hurt me a bit. In fact, they are removing some of my rust spots. Of course, I'm eventually going to need to polish out the scratches from the thorns to look my shiny best."

The Scarecrow, on the other hand, didn't have any trouble with the thorns, except that every once in a while he needed to replace some straw that had become caught and pulled out of his clothes.

The Lion could still pick up Dorothy and Toto's scent, so he knew they were on the right track. "We are lost, but we are making good time," he chuckled.

At least they were certain they hadn't traveled this way before. The thornbushes certainly would have been remembered by all.

The Game Room
of Knarf

The group was very happy when they came upon a small, circular clearing in the middle of the thornbushes.

Jumping off the Tin Woodman's shoulders, the Lion looked toward the early morning sun and said, "This appears to be a good place to stop and rest and check our bearings."

The Tin Woodman carefully extinguished the torch and said, "I wonder why this clearing is right here in the middle of a thorn field? There doesn't seem to be any reason for it."

He relaxed and let his ax fall to the ground. Instead of the muffled sound of the ax hitting dirt, it made the clinking sound of metal against metal. As soon as the ax hit, the ground below them moved and began to lower, knocking them off-balance.

The Lion regained his footing and instinctively, with a mighty leap, jumped to the surface above. The platform continued its descent. The Lion found himself in a tough situation. He did not want to leave his friends to some unknown fate as they dropped lower and lower into the

ground upon the circular platform. But he also didn't know if he would be more help if he stayed safely on the surface.

Finally, the Lion decided that he could not possibly leave his friends by themselves. They needed each other, as a team. He jumped back down onto the platform, landing with a thud and narrowly missing the Scarecrow.

"Good to see you back," said the Tin Woodman.

The round platform continued to move slowly downward. The three friends wondered what would happen next. They tried to climb out, but the walls of the shaft felt like glass.

Suddenly, the platform stopped. They found themselves surrounded by four lighted alcoves, each fronted with thick glass. The Wicked Witch of the West sat on a throne behind the thick glass of the alcove facing them. The Wicked Witch of the East sat in the alcove behind them. The Good Witch of the South and the Good Witch of the North sat on thrones in the two remaining alcoves.

"You have a choice to make, my dear friends," cackled the Wicked Witch of the East. "You may enter any one of these alcoves and the passageway behind it. One of the passageways will help you find Dorothy and Toto. The other three will not, and you will be lost forever." She stood up and straightened her black dress. "But first, let me warn you that what you see is not necessarily what you get."

"Can we ask questions?" inquired the Scarecrow.

"Yes, but you have only one final choice. And let me add, a witch that

appears good may be evil, and an evil witch might be good. None of us may be what we seem.

"Now you may present your questions to us. You have only five minutes. Remember, things may not be what they appear, and our answers to your questions may not be truthful.

"When you make your final decision, you must touch the opening you have chosen, and then the glass will rise. You must then enter the passageway and follow it wherever it leads.

"You three—Lion, Scarecrow, and Tin Woodman—have entered the Game Room of Knarf. You must play the game, whether you like it or not.

"But Knarf is fair. If you solve the game, you will be free to leave."

"Let the game begin," announced a deep voice that must have been Knarf's. The voice echoed around the walls.

The Scarecrow said, "If we are ever going to get out of here to help Dorothy and Toto, we absolutely must choose correctly."

The Lion cleared his voice and faced Glinda, the Good Witch of the South. Glinda sat comfortably upon her throne.

"Are you really the Good Witch of the South?"

"Of course I am, as you can plainly see."

"Do you remember how you saved us from the poppy fields when the Wicked Witch cast a sleeping spell upon us while we were attempting to reach the Emerald City?" asked the Lion.

Glinda, if it was actually her, hesitated a moment before answering. "I caused it to snow, and that broke the spell."

"That is correct," confirmed the Lion.

The Scarecrow noticed that Glinda had hesitated before answering the Lion's question. She should have quickly known the answer to such a simple question, because Glinda knows all by her Great Book of Records.

Next, the Scarecrow faced the Good Witch of the North and asked, "Good Witch of the North, please tell me, what did you do to protect Dorothy?"

"I gave her a kiss on her forehead. No one would hurt a person who has been kissed by the Good Witch of the North, or the Good Witch of the South, for that matter."

"That is true," said the Scarecrow. "That is just the way Dorothy told me it happened."

Next, the Tin Woodman faced the Wicked Witch of the East and asked, "Aren't you supposed to be dead? Didn't Dorothy's farmhouse fall on you in the Munchkin Village?"

"Yes, that dreadful girl's house fell on me," said the witch. "And most people think I was killed—maybe I am dead. Remember, here in the Game Room of Knarf, nothing is what it seems."

"Well," said the Tin Woodman, "if you were really killed by the farmhouse, that would be true. But yet, you are here."

"Yes, I am here," acknowledged the old witch in a sarcastic voice.

"I bet you were upset when your slippers were removed."

"Yes, I was, and I still am," came the reply.

Everything checks out, thought the Tin Woodman, *except she shouldn't be alive.*

Finally, they turned to the Wicked Witch of the West.

"Are you really the Wicked Witch of the West?" asked the Lion.

"Of course I am," she sweetly answered.

"Do you like water?" asked the Lion.

"Of course," came the reply, "as long as none spills on me."

The Lion, the Scarecrow, and the Tin Woodman thought for a minute.

"It seems we have a predicament," said the Scarecrow.

"Yes," said the Tin Woodman.

"We most certainly have," said the Lion. "Since nothing may appear as it should, there is a good chance one of the so-called Wicked Witches could be a Good Witch. And anyway, both of the Wicked Witches are dead. At least, I'm sure one of them is. Everyone believes they are both dead. However, I don't like how Glinda hesitated when I questioned her."

The Scarecrow said, "The passageway behind the Good Witch of the South might be the best chance for us to locate Dorothy and Toto. Wait— let me ask the Good Witch of the North one last question."

Time was running short. The Scarecrow turned to the Good Witch of the North. "Who advised Dorothy to go to the Emerald City to ask the Wizard for help to find her way back to Kansas?"

"I did," came the reply.

"How did you know to tell her that?"

"I used my magic slate."

"Well then, what exactly did the slate say?"

"It said, 'Let Dorothy go to the City of Emeralds.'"

"That is true. Very few people would know that."

The three friends huddled together. They had to make the right decision, or all could be lost.

"Now let's vote on which door to travel through," said the Scarecrow.

The vote was unanimous. The Tin Woodman slowly approached the glass door in front of the Good Witch of the North. He raised his metal hand and knocked gently, just as they were told to do once they had made their decision.

The heavy glass door began to rise slowly.

The Good Witch of the North gave her most gracious smile of welcome. The other witches seemed genuinely upset that the group had not picked them.

Suddenly, the voice of Knarf warned once more, "Remember, nothing may be as it seems." As his voice trailed off, the other three alcoves went dark.

The Tunnels
of Knarf

The Good Witch of the North stepped back to let the the Lion, the Scarecrow, and the Tin Wodman inside the alcove. As soon as they were inside, the heavy glass door slammed down with an ominous thud.

"I hope this is the best choice," said the Scarecrow. "If it is, hopefully we'll be back on Dorothy and Toto's trail very soon."

The Good Witch of the North looked at the three friends and smiled an unusually crooked smile—for her—and with a puff of smoke, she vanished. As the smoke cleared, a panel raised at the back of the alcove, revealing a dark tunnel. The tunnel was nearly six feet wide and was slightly higher than the top of the Tin Woodman's oilcan hat.

The walls of the tunnel glowed a dull green, allowing just enough light for the three of them to find their way.

The Tin Woodman went in first, with his ax in hand. He took each step slowly and carefully along the dimly lit tunnel. Suddenly, he yelled, "Stop, everyone!" He had come to a place where the floor of the tunnel dropped into darkness.

Unfortunately, the Lion couldn't stop in time to avoid running into the Tin Woodman, and he bumped into his friend at the edge of the opening.

The Tin Woodman twirled his arms as he tried to keep himself from falling into the dark and ominous hole, but his tin body wasn't very limber, and he began to lose his balance and fall. "Help! Help!" he yelled.

Using all his cat skills, the Lion instinctively snapped a paw outward and upward. He caught the Tin Woodman—who was dangling precariously over the crevasse—by his arm, and with all his feline might, he yanked him back to safety.

"Are you all right?" the Lion asked. "I'm sorry I bumped into you."

"Yes, I'm fine. You saved me from falling. I would surely have been smashed to bits if you hadn't reacted so quickly."

"I wonder how deep it is?" questioned the Scarecrow. "Let's find out."

The Scarecrow picked up a stone. "There is one way to find out how deep it is. I'm going to drop the stone into the opening and count the seconds until we hear it hit bottom, so everyone be quiet."

The Scarecrow dropped the stone into the opening and counted, "One, two, three. . . ."

The Lion and the Tin Woodman listened to the Scarecrow count as they waited for the stone to hit the bottom of the abyss.

"Ten, eleven, twelve, thirteen, fourteen. . . ."

They still had not heard the stone hit the bottom. Finally, when he reached twenty seconds, the Scarecrow stopped counting. "I don't think this opening has a bottom!" he exclaimed.

In the green glow of the cave walls, everyone merely stared at each other. They were thinking of how to safely cross the opening. If what Knarf said was true, they could not turn back.

Finally, the Lion said, "I think I can jump over it. Though the opening is large, if I can get a running start, I'm sure I will be able to jump across. If I clear the opening far enough, I can carry each of you across on my back, one at a time."

"What if you miss the other side?" asked the Scarecrow. "You would never survive such a fall."

"Probably not," said the Lion. "But do we really have a choice?"

They looked at each other in the eerie green glow of the tunnel. Frankly, no one had another idea on how to get across the abyss. But they worried that even the Lion, with all his strength and agility, couldn't leap across such a distance.

"Well, here goes nothing," said the Lion, as he backed up to get a running start.

The Scarecrow and the Tin Woodman stepped aside.

"Here I go," yelled the Lion as he flew past. When he reached the edge of the abyss, he jumped.

It seemed like an eternity before he landed safely on the other side. Everyone let out a sigh of relief.

"Now what do we do?" asked the Tin Woodman. "You made it, but I don't think either one of us could possibly jump across," he said, pointing to the Scarecrow.

"Now that I know I can make it across," the Lion yelled back, "I think I can carry each of you, one at a time, and still clear the opening."

Now the Lion had to jump back across the abyss. He took a few steps backward and then ran with all his might, pushing off with his powerful hind legs when he reached the opening.

The Lion flew through the air, but as he came down, he realized he had not given himself enough running room to make it all the way across. To everyone's horror, he landed against the edge of the opening. He quickly tried to get a grip on the ground with his front paws, but the dirt kept giving way.

The Tin Woodman and the Scarecrow rushed to their friend. The Tin Woodman grabbed one of the Lion's paws just before he slipped over the edge. The Scarecrow grabbed the Tin Woodman to help him pull the Lion up and out of the hole. Together they strained to pull the Lion up, and they soon had him safely on the ground.

"Thank you," said the Lion. "That was a close call. However, for all of us to cross, I still must carry each of you over. There is no other choice.

"I think it would be best for Dorothy and Toto if I first carry the Scarecrow across, since he is the lightest. Therefore, if something goes wrong, he can continue to look for them."

The Tin Woodman and the Scarecrow agreed.

This time the Lion backed farther into the cave, and with the Scarecrow hugging tightly to his back, he ran harder and faster than before. As he reached the edge of the abyss, he jumped—and made it to the other side with the Scarecrow safe and sound. Then the Lion jumped back across the treacherous gap.

It was now the Tin Woodman's turn. Both the Lion and the Tin Woodman walked backward from the abyss.

"Wait," said the Tin Woodman. "There is one thing I can do to lighten the load." He walked quickly back to the edge of the large opening and tossed his metal ax and his precious oilcan hat across to the other side.

The Scarecrow lent all the encouragement he could. "You will make it across," he yelled.

The Tin Woodman walked back to the Lion. Without hesitation, he climbed up onto the Lion's back and placed his arms tightly around the Lion's neck. "I'm ready, if you are," he said.

The Lion prepared for the feat, digging his hind paws into the dirt for traction. "Here we go," he cried out, and then he bolted toward the opening, with the heavy Tin Woodman holding on as tightly as he could.

The Lion knew that he could make it. He used his love for Dorothy and Toto to give him courage, and he gathered all of his strength for the jump.

When the Lion reached the opening, he leaped into the air. After what seemed like minutes, they landed on the other side, knocking the Scarecrow over and sending him tumbling down the tunnel. The Scarecrow was more than happy to be knocked over, knowing that his friends had safely made it across the opening.

After the Scarecrow brushed himself off, they were ready to continue on their way. As they walked, the Tin Woodman said, "I guess we will

never be able to really tell if something here is real or not, like that open pit. I think we need to assume that everything is real."

The tunnel widened as they moved on, until the three of them could walk side by side. As they carefully moved forward, they saw in the dim light three others walking toward them. The three friends stopped to get a better look. The others stopped at the same time. That's when they realized that the others standing across from them were their exact doubles.

Nobody moved. They just stood there, staring at each other. After a while, the Tin Woodman said, "Enough is enough. Let's run toward them as fast as we can—that should scare these imposters."

The Lion, the Tin Woodman, and the Scarecrow ran down the tunnel toward their doubles. The doubles ran toward them. Closer and closer they approached each other.

They were almost upon each other when the Lion yelled, "Stop! Halt!" All six of them stopped in their tracks.

The three friends could not believe their eyes. In front of them stood another Lion, another Scarecrow, and another Tin Woodman.

The Scarecrow raised his right hand into the air. The Scarecrow facing him did the same.

The Lion made a funny face, and the Lion facing him made the exact funny face.

The Tin Woodman raised his ax high over his head, and the other Tin Woodman did the same.

"It's a mirror that has us fooled," said the Tin Woodman. "It's just a mirror." He was about to bring his ax blade down to break the mirror, because it was standing in their way and they would need to get by it sooner or later.

"Wait!" said the Scarecrow. "Remember that things may not be as they seem in this eerie place."

The Tin Woodman froze with his ax straight up in the air, and then he slowly lowered it and placed it down by his side.

The Lion put his right paw high in the air. His mirror image, standing in front of him, did the same. The Lion took a step toward the mirror and placed his paw on it. His reflection did the same. "It certainly seems to be a mirror," he said. "At least it looks and feels like one."

"Yes, I would agree," said the Scarecrow, "except for one thing. When you and Tin Woodman talk, notice that their mouths don't move. If it really were a mirror, you would see their mouths move. Of course, my mouth doesn't move, because it's just painted on."

The Lion and the Tin Woodman stared at the mirror. The Tin Woodman looked at himself in the mirror and said, "Hello, Tin Woodman."

The mouth of the Tin Woodman in the mirror didn't move.

"Look at the things behind us in the mirror," the Lion said. "Shouldn't a mirror reflect exactly what is in front of it?"

"Well, of course it should," answered the Tin Woodman. "But this one doesn't seem to."

Just then, the three look-alikes, who probably realized they had been discovered, turned and ran down the dimly lit passageway.

"Let's get them," yelled the Lion.

"Yes, let's catch them," echoed the Tin Woodman.

The Lion, who could run the fastest, led the way, followed by the Tin Woodman and finally the Scarecrow, who could barely keep up. After running a short distance, they reached an apparent dead end. The look-alikes were nowhere in sight.

"Don't look behind you," said the Lion.

The three friends turned around, and there, just a few yards away, stood the imposters.

"I can catch them this time," roared the Lion.

"Stop," said the Scarecrow look-alike.

The Lion stopped in his tracks. "You can talk?"

"Yes, I can," said the imitation Scarecrow. "We had fun teasing the three of you, but now the fun is over."

"What do you mean?" asked the Tin Woodman.

The Tin Woodman and the Scarecrow stepped up to stand with the Lion.

"We are only here to confuse you. It is part of the game."

"Then why are you telling us this?"

"Because we always give those who enter Knarf's Game fair warning. It wouldn't be as much fun for us if we did it any other way.

"Remember, follow the Red Brick Road, and it will help lead you to Dorothy and Toto."

"The Red Brick Road?" asked the Scarecrow. "Now, where have I heard of the Red Brick Road?"

Before the Scarecrow could get an answer, a blinding light pierced the darkness of the cave. When the darkness returned, the imposters were gone, but the Lion, the Scarecrow, and the Tin Woodman now noticed two more tunnels, one leading to their left, one to their right. The imposters gave them no clue as to which one would lead to the Red Brick Road.

"I bet any direction we take will be fraught with danger or distraction," said the Tin Woodman. "In that sense, it really doesn't matter which way we go. We'll find the right way out by ourselves, and find Dorothy and Toto too. Isn't that the way we've always done things, as a team?"

"Right you are," the Lion replied. "Put 'em up, put 'em up   I'm ready for anything." He raised his clenched paws in the air.

"Let's go down the passageway to the left," suggested the Scarecrow. "We have nothing to lose—at least, I don't think we do."

"One way for us is as good as another, at this point," observed the Lion. "I'm ready for anything," he repeated.

Off to the left the three went, hoping upon hope that they would soon find the way out of the Tunnels of Knarf.

"It seems there is trouble everywhere around this place," observed the Tin Woodman. "I wonder how Dorothy and Toto are."

"Poor Dorothy and Toto," lamented the Lion. "She should never have left the Yellow Brick Road."

A Way Out

As the Lion, the Scarecrow, and the Tin Woodman moved forward, the tunnel remained illuminated from the green glow magically radiating from the walls, ceiling, and floor. The walls of the tunnel were like glass, smooth and slick to the touch. This was not an ordinary cave with tunnels. Something or someone had made it.

The trio walked carefully, trying their best to avoid trouble. After a few moments, they entered a huge room. A thick fog covered the floor, wrapping around their knees as they walked into the cavern.

Forbidding dark clouds gathered above their heads. Lightning flashed throughout the room, randomly striking the floor and the walls.

One lightning bolt hit the end of the Lion's tail, singing it with a puff of smoke. Fortunately, it only singed his hair and didn't hurt anything except his pride. "Boy! That was close," he yelled.

"If the lightning hits me, I could catch on fire and burn up," said the Scarecrow, as he worriedly looked up at the menacing clouds and flashes of lightning.

"If the lightning hits me, it would move around and through me, since

I'm made of metal. And what would happen to my heart?" questioned the Tin Woodman.

"This place is very strange," said the Scarecrow. "With all this fog, it's like we're outside, near the ocean. Maybe we should find a way out of here."

The three friends looked for a way out of the room. They saw an opening in the wall, glowing green like the tunnel that led them there.

"There's another tunnel," said the Lion. "Let's see if it will lead us out of this place."

As the Lion, the Scarecrow, and the Tin Woodman walked toward the tunnel opening, the head of a huge serpent rose from the mist of the cave and then quickly disappeared. The friends looked at each other in surprise.

"Let's get out of here!" yelled the Lion.

They started toward the tunnel, but the serpent appeared again from beneath the low fog, directly in front of them, blocking their way. The Tin Woodman swung his ax at the serpent, but he missed the beast.

Blue and red fire shot at them from the serpent's open mouth. The Tin Woodman jumped in front of his friends and blocked the flame. His metal body was able to absorb the heat, saving his friends from injury.

The Lion, the Scarecrow, and the Tin Woodman turned and ran as fast as they could. The serpent rose from the fog and moved to cut them off.

Now the friends could see all of the frightening beast. Huge, deep red eyes glowed from his massive head. Large green scales covered his body, and his long tail flipped back and forth in the fog. His legs ended with huge talons larger than an elephant's foot.

The serpent reached out to claw the Lion. The Lion sprang up onto the serpent's long neck and began to claw at the beast's tough scales. The serpent shook his head from side to side, trying to throw the Lion from his neck.

Then the fearsome beast reared back on his tail, exposing the soft underside of his neck. The Tin Woodman saw his opportunity, raised his ax, and swung, cutting the serpent. The serpent disappeared below the foggy mist with a terrible roar as the lightning continued to flash and strike around them.

"Let's go!" yelled the Scarecrow. They ran toward the tunnel as fast as they could, running inside when they reached the opening. They hurried down the passageway, making several turns as they tried to find a way out of the underground maze.

The Sign Maker Returns

The three friends were running down the passageway when the Tin Woodman cried out, "I think I see a light! This way!"

They ran down the tunnel toward the light, and suddenly, amazingly, they were back outside in the forest. They stopped and looked at each other.

"We did it," said the Lion. "I don't know how we did it, but we did."

As soon as he finished his sentence, the Sign Maker appeared. He stopped and said, "Howdy, Lion, good to see ye again."

"Good to see you," answered the Lion. "These are my friends, Scarecrow and Tin Woodman."

"Greetings. Nice to meet ye," the Sign Maker replied.

"How are things going?" the Lion asked his old acquaintance. "Have you posted many signs lately?"

"I've posted a few here and there," the Sign Maker replied, "but, unfortunately, I'm not always able to help people the way I would like, because of the Wicked Witch of the West."

"The Wicked Witch of the West!" exclaimed the Scarecrow.

"Yes, she is still alive," explained the Sign Maker. "No one really knows how, but she has come back and now wants to rule Oz. However, she is small, like a tiny doll. But don't let that fool you—her powers are growing strong.

"I warn you, if you follow Dorothy and Toto, you could fall into the same predicament they did. If you enter the area called Never Return, you won't be able to leave. Then all of you, like Dorothy and Toto, will be captured."

"But you apparently come and go from Never Return," the Scarecrow observed intelligently.

"That is true. Evidently, I am more useful to the Wicked Witch if I'm allowed to roam."

"You could be useful to us, by sending us in the direction of Never Return," stated the Scarecrow.

"Follow me," the Sign Maker said.

With the help of the Sign Maker, they reached the Red Brick Road before long.

"The Red Brick Road!" exclaimed the Tin Woodman. "There really is a Red Brick Road after all."

The Sign Maker reached into his bag of signs, pulled one out, and stuck the pole into the soft forest ground. "To find Dorothy and Toto, follow the Red Brick Road this way," he said, pointing them in the direction of Never Return. As he said the words, they magically appeared on the sign itself, along with an arrow pointing the way.

The Lion, the Scarecrow, and the Tin Woodman just stood and looked at each other.

"You're not playing one of your tricks, are you?" asked the Lion.

"I wouldn't do that," answered the Sign Maker with a serious expression. "Well, I must be on my way again. There are many signs that need posting." With that said, the Sign Maker turned and waved goodbye.

The Lion, the Scarecrow, and the Tin Woodman waved back at the Sign Maker. They could hear him singing his usual song as he rounded a curve in the Red Brick Road:

> Oh, I'm the Sign Maker,
> I'm the Sign Maker.
> Follow my signs,
> and you will find,
> you're never left behind.
> No, you're never left behind.

Soon both he and his song faded into the distance.

A Stop
for the Night

The Lion, the Scarecrow, and the Tin Woodman stood upon the strange Red Brick Road in the middle of the forest.

"Which way should we go?" asked the Lion. "The Sign Maker is very sly. Should we go in the opposite direction he advised, or should we travel in the direction he suggested?"

The Scarecrow's brain was buzzing. You could almost hear him thinking. Finally, he said, "I think this time I would follow the sign's instructions. I have a hunch about this. If what the Sign Maker said is true, then maybe the Wicked Witch has Dorothy. And if she has Dorothy, then we need to find her. If we find the witch, then we'll find Dorothy. It's worth a shot, at least."

The Lion and the Tin Woodman agreed with the Scarecrow.

"Finally, we can be on our way again," said the Tin Woodman. "But who knows what is up ahead?"

The Lion sniffed the ground. "It looks like I've lost Dorothy's scent. I'll keep trying."

"Poor Dorothy. Poor Toto," sighed the Scarecrow.

Time passed slowly in the forest. The flutter of leaves from the cool breeze caused the sunlight to hypnotically travel back and forth upon the Red Brick Road.

The roots of the trees alongside the road had grown their way under it and had, over the years, caused the bricks to rise. Judging from its disrepair, the Red Brick Road must have been laid a long time ago. But why did the road exist at all?

Most in Oz knew that the Red Brick Road started next to the Yellow Brick Road. But somewhere in time it had evidently lost its usefulness, and it was now overgrown and in disrepair as it meandered outside of Munchkin Land. Indeed, there were places where the road completely disappeared from years and years of weather and lack of care.

Outside the land of the Munchkins, the road had become just a memory. For all intents and purposes, it just stopped at the edge of the town square. Yet, here it was, as the Lion, the Tin Woodman, and the Scarecrow stumbled their way over its cracks and humps. To some degree, the forest had been kinder to the road, because the forest canopy gave it at least some protection.

Here and there, a spear of sunlight found an opening through the forest shade, lighting the way for the three friends as they journeyed in search of Dorothy and Toto.

It seemed like they had walked for miles. The road twisted and turned through the eerie forest. After some time, they noticed that the spears of light had started to dim.

"Soon it will be night," said the Tin Woodman. "We'd better find a place for Lion to sleep."

"That is kind of you to consider my needs," commented the Lion, "since neither of you require sleep."

"Yes, that is certainly true," acknowledged the Scarecrow. "I do not need sleep at all. In fact, as you well know, I couldn't close my eyes to sleep even if I wanted to, since they are just painted on my gunnysack face."

"Since I'm made from metal, I do not need to sleep either," said the Tin Woodman. "Although sometimes it is nice to just sit to my heart's desire."

"Yet," said the Lion, "it is nice to have you consider my needs to eat and sleep."

By this time, twilight had passed and night was upon them. They decided it would be wise to move to one side of the Red Brick Road to stop and wait for morning. If they stayed on the road, there's no telling what people or creatures might come upon them in the dark.

"Maybe we should find a place to stay off of the road," said the Scarecrow. "I don't think we'd want to meet something we couldn't see."

The Lion and the Tin Woodman agreed, so they hurried off the road. After a moment of searching, they found a wide opening in the hollow trunk of a very, very large tree. The opening led into a place big enough to fit all three of them quite comfortably for the night.

Soon they were happy that they were protected from the elements. They could hear the howl of the wind through the forest—at least, they thought it was the wind.

It seemed, at times, they could also hear things moving along the Red Brick Road. But since the opening in the tree faced away from the road and since no one particularly wanted to leave their cozy quarters to try to discover the source of the sounds in the darkness, everyone was quite comfortable to stay right where they were.

The Lion finally fell asleep.

The Tin Woodman placed himself near the opening in the tree trunk, his ax at the ready, just in case something unsavory decided to join them.

The sounds along the Red Brick Road continued for a few hours and then stopped.

The Lion woke up and yawned. "Nights sure are long around here," he said.

"They sure are," agreed the Tin Woodman. "Now that the strange sounds have stopped, I think I'll go outside to look around. The tree opening should be right about here." He hit the area where the opening was, but his ax struck nothing but hard wood. "It's so dark, I can't find the opening. I was sitting right next to it, and now I can't find it."

"We'll find it in the morning," said the Scarecrow.

"I'm not too sure. It feels like morning," observed the Lion. "I know I slept quite a while, and besides, it didn't seem this dark when we first came inside."

"I have an idea, Lion," said the Tin Woodman. "You stay where you are, and I'll feel around the perimeter of the tree trunk until I feel the opening."

The Tin Woodman found the Lion and then began to feel his way around the inside of the tree trunk. In the dark, he stumbled across the Scarecrow. "Sorry," the Tin Woodman said to his friend.

"That's okay," answered the Scarecrow. "You can't hurt straw."

Finally, the Tin Woodman completed the entire inner circumference of the tree. He didn't find an opening, but he did find a step. He felt a little higher and found another step above it. Then he reached even higher, and sure enough, there was a third step and then a fourth.

The Lion and the Scarecrow found the Tin Woodman in the dark and followed him up the inside of the tree. The group decided they had nothing to lose by discovering where the stairs led. They wondered why they hadn't noticed the stairs when they first entered the tree trunk, but, of course, it had been quite dark outside and particularly dark inside the old tree.

"This tree must be hundreds of years old," commented the Scarecrow. "It is huge."

The Tin Woodman led the way up the stairs, which grew from the tree itself. Finally, they reached a platform with a ladder resting on it. They carefully traveled up the ladder.

At one point, they came to an opening in the trunk that led outside. They could see daylight. They crawled, one at a time, through the opening toward the light.

"If we go much higher, we will be above all the other trees in this forest," observed the Lion.

"Well, so far," said the Scarecrow, "I don't see any alternative for us but to keep moving. The stairs and this opening must be here for a reason."

"Yeah, I hope it is for a good reason," said the Tin Woodman. "I don't like that we couldn't go out the same way we came in."

"It seems very suspicious to me," remarked the Lion.

Finally, they reached the outer opening of the passageway, where they moved out into the open. The large branches of the tree spread out in all directions.

Just above them, at the very top of the tree, perched an elaborate tree house. The tree house had been carefully constructed, with braces anchoring it to the strong thick branches below it. The stairs continued again in the open until they reached the porch of the tree house. The porch circled the entire house.

The three friends climbed the remaining stairs to the porch of the tree house. It felt good to be out in the sunlight. They could see for miles in all directions, over the tops of the rest of the trees in the forest. Far below them, they could see a patch of the Red Brick Road at the base of the tree trunk. In the distance, they could see what appeared to be water, perhaps a lake.

"I hope whoever lives here is friendly," said the Lion.

They walked around the porch. The house had large windows on each side, but it was too dark inside for them to see into the house. They found the door on the far side.

The only sound came from the wind brushing the tree's blue-green

leaves. All three stood before the thick wooden door.

"I guess we'd better knock," advised the Tin Woodman. He took the flat end of his ax and tapped gently three times, but no one answered. He tried once again, this time tapping a little harder and a little louder, and again no one answered.

The Lion glanced over his shoulder above the porch railing; his keen sight had spotted something in the distance. Far out in the sky was a black dot. The dot became larger as it came closer to them. The three turned their complete attention to the object that was heading their way. It became increasingly obvious that it was a very large bird.

"Look! Look!" yelled the Lion.

The Tin Woodman and the Scarecrow watched as the bird flew ever closer. They suddenly realized that this was not an ordinary bird. In fact, it was not a bird at all.

The image quickly became all too familiar. To their amazement, they saw that it was the Wicked Witch of the West on her broomstick! She was flying right for them.

"The door!" yelled the Lion. "Hurry, let's get inside—she's coming closer!"

Suddenly, all possible fear of what could be inside the tree house left them. The Tin Woodman quickly turned the door handle, and the door easily swung open. The three rushed inside and closed the door behind them. They ran to one of the large windows just as the Wicked Witch flew by.

The Wicked Witch circled the tree house once, cackling her vicious laugh all the while. Then she came to an abrupt stop in midair just outside the door.

"Well, well, well," she shrieked, "I guess I'll be on my way. At first, I thought I would have to go to the trouble of taking care of the three of you myself, but now I guess I won't have to.

"By the way, I thought you would like to know, Dorothy and Toto are okay—at least for now. Have fun in your tree house." She cackled menacingly as she rode off on her broom.

The three friends all breathed a sigh of relief when the Wicked Witch disappeared from view. Now that she had flown out of sight, they turned from the window.

The Lion said, "I wonder what she meant by her comment that she wouldn't have to take care of us now."

"Maybe we are trapped here," the Scarecrow replied.

"Let me try the door," the Tin Woodman said as he walked over and reached for the door handle. He tried to open the door, but it wouldn't budge. "It looks like we *are* trapped in this tree house."

Knowing they couldn't leave, they took a moment to look at their surroundings. The tree house was completely bare, without a stick of furniture, or anything else, for that matter.

Realizing they were trapped, the friends sat down upon the hard wooden floor, facing each other with their backs against the walls.

It was just a little disconcerting to have seen the Wicked Witch again,

after all this time, alive and apparently well. She was supposed to have melted away to nothing.

The Scarecrow suggested that maybe they had imagined the witch.

"She looked very real to me," said the Lion.

"Me too," said the Tin Woodman. "Let's hope we never see her again."

Splinter

The tree house was dark and cold. The wind had increased, and the tree house swayed back and forth with the tree.

Suddenly, in the dark, a voice said, "Welcome to my tree house. You'll have to excuse me—it is a little bare without pictures and furniture, but it does have a nice view. Don't you think?"

"Who is that?" asked the Lion. "Who is that?"

"Silly me," said the voice, "I forget that people and creatures get a little confused. It is me, the tree."

"You mean to say that you—the tree—are talking?"

"I am certainly a tree, and it is true, I am talking."

The Scarecrow cleared his throat. "I've rarely heard of a tree that talked, except the Apple Trees alongside the Yellow Brick Road."

"Yep, I talk, and I grew the tree house myself."

"Let me get this straight," said the Tin Woodman. "You, as a tree, grew this house?"

"Yes. You might say I grew it myself. You see, the house is just another part of me. Just like my roots and leaves."

"But why did you grow a tree house?" asked the Tin Woodman.

"I decided it would be a nice place for visitors to stay and enjoy the view," replied the tree.

"It is nice, and we thank you," said the Scarecrow. "Did you by any chance close the opening in your trunk so we could not leave the way we came in?"

"My, you are a brilliant fellow," said the tree in a most sincere voice.

"I gather you would prefer that we stay here a while," said the Scarecrow.

"That is partially true," said the tree. "Actually, I want you to stay here forever. You can be my friends and share my view from the tree house."

"It is quite a view," said the Tin Woodman, acknowledging the tree while at the same time attempting to humor it. "Now I see why the Wicked Witch said she wouldn't have to bother with us."

"Have you had any other visitors?" asked the Tin Woodman.

"Oh, yes, from time to time," said the tree in a sorrowful voice. "But they are all gone. It seems no one ever stays long enough to really get to know me. I get so lonely without someone to talk with."

"What about the other trees?" asked the Lion.

"Very few trees can talk. It is just poor me around here."

"May I ask you two questions?" asked the Scarecrow.

"Sure you can," the tree answered in a friendly voice.

"First, do you have a name, and second, how come you grew so tall compared to the rest of the trees in this forest?"

"My name is Splinter. I was cared for by the Tree Elves, and that is the reason I can talk and why I grew so very tall. The Tree Elves gave me the power to speak. They watered me daily and fed my soil with all kinds of nourishing things. I just grew taller and taller, and after some time, I was much taller than all the other trees of the forest."

"Where are the Tree Elves now?" asked the Scarecrow.

"I don't know. One morning they all went away. I grew this tree house especially for them to live in. I wanted to thank them for all of their care and give them their very own place to stay—a place they could call home.

"But go away they did. Even the Sign Maker, who happened to walk by one day, couldn't help me. Even he didn't know where the Tree Elves had gone."

"That is bad," said the Scarecrow, "because the Sign Maker knows an awful lot about where things are."

"So, here I am, alone, except I now have the three of you in my tree house instead of the Tree Elves."

The Tin Woodman was almost afraid to ask, but he did. "May I ask, what happened to the others? There must have been others that climbed up to the tree house and went in."

"Oh, they would stay a while. They would walk around the porch, of course, but they couldn't climb back down because the stairs would be removed. Eventually, they would just leave," said Splinter.

The Lion asked, "But how could they leave without the stairs?"

"They would try to climb down my tree limbs and trunk," explained

Splinter. "Naturally, I couldn't allow that, so I would just shake and shake until they fell."

"That was not very nice," said the Scarecrow.

"I guess not," said Splinter, "but it wasn't good of them to leave my nice tree house and leave me all alone."

The three friends walked around the porch until they were at the point where the stairs had been. Sure enough, the stairs were gone, and they were trapped.

The Lion, the Scarecrow, and the Tin Woodman stayed in the tree house at night and walked around the porch during the day. They were hoping to devise a plan of escape. Sometimes they would chat with Splinter, but after three days, they had little left to talk about, except the weather. Nonetheless, Splinter was pleased to have them as company.

While the Tin Woodman and the Scarecrow were in good shape, the Lion had not eaten for some time, and he was very thirsty. Something had to be done soon.

"You know," said the Scarecrow, "if we could locate the Tree Elves, perhaps then Splinter would let us go."

"I would let you go," interrupted Splinter, "although I would still miss you." Splinter was pleasant in his conversations. It almost seemed as though he didn't know the consequences of his actions by keeping them trapped.

The Scarecrow kept wondering why the Tree Elves would leave Splinter so suddenly. It made the poor tree so alone with no one to talk with.

Also, why did the Tree Elves give so much attention and care to him while apparently ignoring the other trees nearby?

The three friends knew that they must do something soon. Each day that they were trapped meant one less day to help Dorothy and Toto. Plus the Lion was getting weaker as his days went by without food and water. He was able to lick some dew from the tree's leaves in the mornings, but that hardly provided enough water to sustain him. He tried the tree's leaves for food, but they were bitter to the taste.

There was little they could do. They figured that they would have to jump, as all had before them, and hope for the best. It was a long, long way down. They decided to sleep on this drastic idea before they put it into action.

That evening, the Scarecrow told the tree that they would probably leave the next day.

Splinter swayed back and forth as if the wind was pushing against him. "No, no. You can't leave. You are my friends," he said.

"Well, friends don't lock other friends up just to keep them company," retorted the Scarecrow.

Splinter stopped swaying. It became very quiet. It was the first time anyone had ever answered him in such a manner. Finally, the giant tree merely said, "I'm sorry."

Then he explained that he could regrow the stairs and unseal the opening at the base of his trunk to let them go, but it would take quite some time to accomplish.

"I'm not certain Lion can wait very much longer without food and water," said the Scarecrow.

"I will start at once. I'm so very, very sorry," repeated Splinter.

The Lion, the Scarecrow, and the Tin Woodman never held a grudge.

"Do your best," pleaded the Scarecrow. "Time is of the essence, particularly for Lion."

Soon night fell. The three friends thought about the next day. They decided to jump from the tree house together, because each was a close friend of the other. They decided they could not wait for Splinter to regrow the stairs.

Splinter's Redemption

The night was unusually dark. The moon was only a silver sliver. A strong wind whistled as it passed through the railings on the porch of the tree house.

Finally, the Lion fell asleep while the Scarecrow and the Tin Woodman waited in the dark, because they didn't need sleep, as everyone knows. They sat on the floor and reminisced about all the things they had been through, both good and bad, and how they had always remained friends.

"Teamwork, that's what it was," said the Tin Woodman.

"And what it is," added the Scarecrow.

"Teamwork and the love of the Tree Elves is why Splinter is such a magnificent tree. Large and beautiful," said the Tin Woodman.

Although the Scarecrow and the Tin Woodman were whispering, Splinter could hear them. He began to cry. The Scarecrow and the Tin Woodman could hear his sobs.

"Why are you crying?" asked the Scarecrow, keeping his voice low so he wouldn't wake the Lion.

"No one has ever called me magnificent and beautiful," Splinter replied. "Indeed, I've been mean. Look how I trapped the three of you here for purely selfish reasons. Just so I can have someone to talk with. No one ever stayed long, and now you will be gone tomorrow. You will jump from my tree house, but I do not blame you."

The Scarecrow asked Splinter, "Can you see?"

"No. My eyes do not work. But I can talk, hear, and feel."

"But how do you know," asked the Tin Woodman, "that there is this beautiful view from your treetop?"

"I know because others have told me how truly beautiful it is."

"I understand," said the Lion, who had awakened moments before and had heard most of the conversation.

"I'm sorry I woke you," said Splinter.

"That is all right," assured the Lion, "I agree with my friends that you are magnificent as well as beautiful. I bet it took a lot of teamwork by the Tree Elves to help you grow so big and beautiful."

"It did," said Splinter. "I just really never appreciated it until now."

Suddenly, a Tree Elf came inside the tree house through the partially opened door. He introduced himself to the Lion, the Scarecrow, and the Tin Woodman. Around his tiny waist was a belt with a tiny silver buckle. The buckle had a tree engraved on it.

"Apparently," the Tree Elf said, "Splinter has learned a valuable lesson. He never understood, until now, how teamwork and love can build or grow into something magnificent, if you really want it to be."

Splinter, as big and strong as he was, could only sob again and meekly answer, "Yes, that is true. And I would do anything to help Lion, Scarecrow, and Tin Woodman."

"Perhaps you can," said the Tree Elf. "You could become a seedling and begin to grow all over again. However, this time, you would need to learn and grow big and strong completely on your own, except of course, we will check on you from time to time. But this time, it will be entirely up to you. Are you willing to start over to save your new friends?"

"I am ready," Splinter replied. "I appreciate you and the rest of the Tree Elves for the chance to do something truly magnificent, to save my new friends and to know all Tree Elves may learn to respect me once more. Now I know why you left so suddenly."

"All right," said the Tree Elf. "Lion, Scarecrow, and Tin Woodman, you will need to go outside and hold on tight to one of Splinter's large limbs. Splinter will begin to shrink, and when you are safely close to the ground, you must jump off. Make sure you jump far enough away from Splinter so you won't be injured and so you don't injure Splinter, because when you see him again, he will be quite small and fragile."

It was hard for the three friends to picture Splinter as a seedling. There was a pause as the three of them left the tree house and climbed carefully onto one of Splinter's large limbs.

Splinter asked one last question. "Can I grow as tall as I am now?"

"You can," said the Tree Elf. "Though it will take some time, and it will be entirely up to you." Then, the Tree Elf added one more thing. "If you succeed on your own and become as magnificent in size and beauty as you are now, not only will you be able to talk, hear, and feel the touch of things, but I promise," said the Tree Elf solemnly, "that you will be able, for the first time, to see. To see the view and all the other things around you."

From outside, the Lion, the Scarecrow, and the Tin Woodman yelled encouragement to Splinter. "You can do it," they all shouted at once.

"Yes, I can," answered Splinter. "It is nice to have you as true friends."

The Tree Elf flew up to the very top of Splinter and touched the tree blazoned upon his magic belt buckle, just as the morning sun peeked over a far mountain.

The Lion, the Scarecrow, and the Tin Woodman held on tight to their branch. Slowly at first, then faster, Splinter began to shrink. His branches and leaves became smaller and smaller as his trunk narrowed and shortened.

"We are close enough to the ground now," yelled the Tin Woodman. "It is almost time to jump. And remember, watch out for Splinter."

The tree limb they were clinging to began to bend under their weight as Splinter continued to shrink. Very soon, the Tin Woodman yelled, "Jump!" All three jumped safely to the forest floor.

The Tin Woodman found his ax nearby. The Scarecrow lost a little straw, which they gathered up and put back into place. "Teamwork!" they all said together.

The Tree Elf was gone. In a small clearing next to the Red Brick

Road, a seedling stood proudly, with a beam of sunlight touching its tiny branches. A seedling by the name of Splinter.

The three friends said good-bye to Splinter. They were not sure whether or not he could hear them. They hoped that they would meet him again someday.

The Scarecrow and the Tin Woodman waited as the Lion bounded into the forest to search for food. He returned a short time later with a full belly and a spring in his step.

Then they turned and headed once again on their journey down the Red Brick Road.

The Three Friends
Enter Never Return

The Red Brick Road made many twists and turns as the three friends moved along. The Lion found a pond nearby and took a well-deserved drink of water. They traveled the road as fast as practical. Eventually, they reached a sign that read:

Do Not Enter This Area.

As they started to move past the sign, they heard a laughing cackle in the distance, a cackle that sounded very much like the Wicked Witch of the West. All three of them froze.

"P-p-perhaps," the Lion stuttered, "perhaps the Wicked Witch really is still alive."

"She can't be," the Tin Woodman whispered. "Dorothy melted her."

"Yeah, yeah, of course, it can't be her. She is gone," agreed the Lion, who was trying to convince himself that the witch was indeed gone forever.

"This whole journey through the forest and down the Red Brick Road is starting to play tricks on us," suggested the Scarecrow. "We are prob-

ROGER S. BAUM

ably just hearing things that are not there. It is, I'm sure, just the sound of the forest, with its animals and the wind passing through the trees."

"Yeah, yeah, hearing things. That's it," said the Lion, who was beginning to sound a bit like the Cowardly Lion of old.

"Teamwork!" yelled the Tin Woodman again.

"Onward!" yelled the Scarecrow.

"Onward!" seconded the Lion.

"Let's keep moving," said the Tin Woodman. "We have to find Dorothy and Toto, warning sign or no warning sign."

The three friends took several more steps beyond the sign that explicitly warned them not to enter the area. Then it happened. Everything around them began to grow taller. The trees became huge, even the plants seemed gigantic. The Red Brick Road seemed wider.

"What's happening?" asked the Tin Woodman. "When I was cutting trees near my cabin in the woods, I never ever saw trees this large, not even one. Some of these trees look almost as tall as Splinter. Why, it would take me a week just to cut down one of these. They are so big."

"Wait a minute," said the Scarecrow, "the trees and everything else around us appear larger because we are smaller. Just look at the Red Brick Road. Look again at how wide it has become, not because of more bricks—each individual brick appears larger. We have shrunk."

"Yes," confirmed the Lion. "The bricks appear larger than they were because we are so much smaller then before."

After they recovered from the initial shock, the Tin Woodman said,

"Well, big or small, short or tall, we must find Dorothy and Toto. We must carry on."

"I agree," said the Scarecrow. "We have to help Dorothy and Toto."

"Onward," said the Lion.

The three brave friends continued their journey. It took them, just as it had taken Dorothy and Toto, much more time to cover the same distance as when they were taller.

They passed the Red Brick Road Village. All three of them looked at the village sign and its record of the village population. The sign was the same one Dorothy had observed, only this time the population said "0."

The Lion asked, "How could someone add a zero if there is no one left in the town to write the zero on the sign?"

The Scarecrow thought a moment. "Maybe the last one to leave did it on his way out of town," he suggested.

They decided not to stop in the deserted town but instead to continue down the Red Brick Road, in order to move along without delay.

The Lion picked up the scent of Dorothy, though the scent was faint. The friends quickened their pace.

Suddenly, they saw a tiny, doll-like person in the middle of the road, blocking their path. It was Bekama! Her guards stood at attention behind her.

"Stop!" Bekama ordered. "Where do you think you're going?"

The Lion, the Scarecrow, and the Tin Woodman came to an immediate halt.

"Who are you?" asked the Lion.

"If you must know who I am, my name is Bekama. I am the ruler of Never Return. Why do you invade our land?"

"We didn't invade anything," the Tin Woodman said. "Our friend is lost, and we are looking for her."

"You are looking for Dorothy and Toto, aren't you?"

"Yes, but how did you know?" replied the Tin Woodman.

"Never mind how I know. Just call it a wild guess," said Bekama.

Although she appeared harmless, Bekama spoke in very harsh tones. Her black eyes added to her devilish look and matched the harshness in her voice.

Suddenly, just as had happened to Dorothy and Toto, the trees and plants and everything else around them appeared to grow even larger than before. The Lion, the Scarecrow, and the Tin Woodman looked at each other and wondered what was happening to them.

Bekama noticed their confusion. "You are in the land of Never Return," she said, "and now you're shrunken, just like the rest of us. You can never leave this land, and you can never regain your former stature.

"Maybe, though, you can find Dorothy and Toto. I will give you a hint. If you follow the Red Brick Road to the water, I think you will be very close to them."

As Bekama finished her sentence, rain began to fall. Her guards put an umbrella over Bekama's head, and they ran out of sight without another word.

The Lion, the Scarecrow, and the Tin Woodman walked through the rain in the direction Bekama recommended. They stopped briefly so the Tin Woodman could carefully oil his joints so he would not rust.

Soon, they reached a body of water that blocked their way. And just like Dorothy had, they could see the Red Brick Road traveling beneath the water's surface.

Eventually, a little boat appeared on the horizon. It came closer and finally docked next to them. The Lion, the Scarecrow, and the Tin Woodman climbed into the little boat. They could see the words "Tugg Jr." on the side of the boat. No one steered the craft, yet it pulled away from the shore under its own power.

The Lion, the Scarecrow, and the Tin Woodman sat aboard Tugg Jr. and watched as they passed over the Red Brick Road. However, they soon noticed that they had turned away from the road, off into the vast lake they floated on. Knowing they could do nothing else, they waited in the boat as night came and darkness fell.

The Lion fell asleep, while the Scarecrow and the Tin Woodman kept watch for land.

The Scarecrow was looking over the side of the boat as the sun came up. "I see land!" he exclaimed.

His voice roused the sleeping Lion.

"And there's the Red Brick Road," said the Tin Woodman. "I guess Tugg Jr. knew where he was going all along."

The three friends waited as Tugg Jr. drifted to shore. When the boat stopped, they disembarked on dry land.

"By the way, Tugg Jr.," asked the Lion, "what do people eat around here? I am so hungry."

"Everyone eats the berries," Tugg Jr. replied. "But you must eat just the green-and-red ones, not the green-and-purple ones. If you eat the green-and-purple berries, something terrible happens—at least, that's what Bekama tells everyone. As I understand it, the green-and-red berries are delicious, and they change flavor with every bite.

"Well, good-bye now. I'll be back on my way to the other shore. There's no telling who will be waiting there for a boat ride."

"Good-bye, Tugg Jr.," said the Tin Woodman. "And thank you for the lift. It is greatly appreciated."

The Scarecrow took a moment and used a piece of his jacket to dry off the Tin Woodman. "We just can't let you rust," he said to his metal friend.

The Lion, the Scarecrow, and the Tin Woodman continued down the Red Brick Road. Before long, they walked up on the old mansion that Dorothy had encountered.

They stopped in front of its door, and the Tin Woodman knocked with his ax to see if someone would answer. When no one came, he knocked again, this time a little louder.

The three friends waited, wondering if someone would answer. Then they heard muffled footsteps coming from inside the mansion, and they saw the doorknob turn. Then the heavy door swung open slowly, its hinges creaking loudly, and there stood a tall, elderly gentleman with a mustache.

"Hello," the gentleman said with a happy grin. "You're lucky I heard you knock. I'm usually in my library. In fact, this place is so large, I rarely travel far. So, here I am, and there you are, my friends."

"Excuse me, but I'm not sure we've met before. I'm the Tin Woodman."

"Well, I must admit that we have met before, but you probably don't remember how. Nonetheless, my name is Frank, and you are the Tin Woodman, as you say, and you are the Lion of Oz, and you are the Scarecrow of Oz." Frank looked at each one and smiled. "I imagine you are looking for Dorothy and Toto. The best way to find them would be to walk around to the backside of this old mansion, where you will find the Red Brick Road. Just stay on it until you reach the Silver Bridge. There I think you will find Dorothy and Toto.

"By the way, watch out for Bekama. She is really the Wicked Witch of the West!"

"The Wicked Witch of the West!" the three friends said in unison.

"That's impossible," said the Scarecrow. "Dorothy melted her."

"Well," said Frank, "that's what most people think. But nothing is impossible in Oz. The Wicked Witch has found a way to come back— perhaps someone wanted her to return, and they helped her."

"Who would want her to come back?" the Lion asked.

"I might know something about that," Frank replied, "but I don't have time to explain it now. You must hurry to the Silver Bridge and help Dorothy and Toto. The Wicked Witch is there, too. Around this mansion you must go, and remember, stay on the Red Brick Road until you reach them. Now go—you must hurry."

The Tin Woodman wanted to ask Frank another question, but the kind gentleman had disappeared behind the closing mansion door.

The Lion, the Scarecrow, and the Tin Woodman looked at each other, and without another word they turned the corner of the building and ran as fast as they could. They found the Red Brick Road, and a short distance ahead they could see the Silver Bridge. They continued to run until they reached it.

PART III

A HAPPY REUNION

Crossing the Silver Bridge

Dorothy decided to make her move. She ran with Toto past the Wicked Witch, but as she reached the far end of the Silver Bridge, she heard a call.

"Dorothy, wait! We made it!"

Her heart jumped at the sound of the voices of the Lion, the Scarecrow, and the Tin Woodman. She stopped and turned. Sure enough, her friends were there. They had found her at last.

"Congratulations," said Bekama. "You are all together again. Naturally, it won't do you any good. No one leaves the land of Never Return until I say so. And right now. . . ." The witch smiled an evil smile. "I don't say so."

The Lion ran as fast as he could toward the tiny Wicked Witch and jumped when he reached her. Just as he was about to wrap his paws around her, she vanished. The Lion hit the bridge with a thud.

With the Wicked Witch gone, the Lion, the Scarecrow, and the Tin Woodman were able to go and greet Dorothy and Toto. They were very happy to have found them unharmed, even though they were a bit small.

The group decided to try to cross to the other side of the Silver Bridge, but they were stopped by the invisible barrier. They could find no way through.

With no need for great haste, all five of them talked a while about their journey. The Tin Woodman told Dorothy about Splinter, and she told her friends about her ride on the branch.

Finally, the Scarecrow said, "We have to get down to business. What is our next move?"

Dorothy thought a moment and then said, "I think there is only one person here who can help us, and her name is Micur. She lives in a large pool in that old mansion. Even if Micur cannot help us, maybe we can help her escape the clutches of the Witched Witch."

The five of them headed back to the mansion. They entered through the rear door and walked into the gloom of the old place.

"I believe Micur and the pool are somewhere near the center of the mansion," Dorothy said. "Let's head in the same direction we are headed now and try to stay close to the walls."

They traveled as best they could in a straight line. The passageways twisted and turned, and it was difficult to go straight to the center of the mansion. They became fascinated by all the doors along the way, but they had no time to explore.

After a long while and with much frustration, they finally found the pool and the mural surrounding it. The stars painted on the mural provided enough light to dimly illuminate the room.

Dorothy was excited. She could hardly wait to hear Micur again. She called out, "Micur! Micur! It's Dorothy. I need to talk with you."

The Lion, the Scarecrow, and the Tin Woodman could only gaze in awe at the beautiful mural. It had everything in Oz on it. Indeed, they could even see themselves painted on the Yellow Brick Road.

Dorothy said, "Micur creates the mural to keep her busy while she hides in the pool. You know how the Wicked Witch hates water."

Slowly, the water in the pool began to drain until all of them could see the crystal globe upon its pedestal. When the water completely disappeared, they walked down the stairs to the bottom of the pool.

When they reached the bottom of the pool, Micur said, "I didn't expect to see you again, or at least, not so soon. I'm overjoyed."

"I'm overjoyed as well," said Dorothy. "These are my friends Lion, Scarecrow, and Tin Woodman."

All three bowed low before the silver globe. By now the globe had risen above the pedestal, as it had when Dorothy first encountered Micur.

"I know the three of you as well as I know Dorothy and Toto," Micur said. "After all, you can see that you are a part of my mural."

"Yes," said the Tin Woodman, "we did notice the honor you have given us by placing us in such a beautiful mural."

"We are here to take you from this place, Micur," said Dorothy. "We all need to leave. We cannot remain in the land of Never Return forever. I'm sure if we work together, we can escape the Wicked Witch and foil her plot to capture the Emerald City."

"Are you sure, Dorothy?" questioned Micur.

"We can't be sure of anything, except the strength of teamwork. I think each of us can give the other help and encouragement. There is no time like the present to try.

"Is there a way we can take you and your globe outside again? If we can get that far, you can join your family in the clouds."

After a long silence, Micur answered, "Yes, let's try together. And once we are outside, I have an idea about what we can do." Micur did not elaborate.

Slowly, the silver globe with Micur inside floated over to Dorothy and gently descended into her basket. The berries were all gone, so the basket had plenty of room for the globe.

The group climbed up the stairs of the pool opposite the way they had entered. As they walked through the door and into the hall, the mural disappeared, along with its stars.

Together they traveled down the twisting passageways of the mansion. In the gloom of the hallways, they heard the Wicked Witch's voice screaming, "It won't do you any good. You cannot leave the land of Never Return. I forbid it. So have your fun." Her wicked cackle resounded in the distance.

The Tin Woodman held his ax high and the Lion's hair stood straight up on his back when they heard the voice of the Wicked Witch.

The Castle in the Clouds

Finally, with good fortune, the group found the rear door to the mansion and ran out into the sunlight.

Dorothy carefully removed the silver globe from her basket.

"It is good to feel the sunlight again," Micur said. "I never thought I would see the sun again as long as the Wicked Witch was around."

Then the globe began to break apart, and there in the center stood the tiny princess. Her dress was silver and her wand was white. Her hair was as white as the clouds above. She wore white shoes with tiny gold bows, and her skin radiated like sunlight.

"I'm free," she said. "I'm free thanks to you, Dorothy, and all of the rest of you as well.

"I told you I had an idea. Dorothy, remember when we talked, and you said you could see things in the clouds, like dogs and cats and faces and trees and all kinds of things?

"And remember, I said that my people help to create those images. That is how I was able to create the mural.

"I can help you leave Never Return, but only for a moment. But each moment counts, so I would like you to meet my family."

Suddenly, a cloud floated down to their feet. Then the cloud shaped itself into a stairway that climbed up into the blue sky. At the top of the stairway was a cloud castle.

"Now, my friends, let's meet my mother and father and all my bothers and sisters and all the rest who would like to thank you for your courage."

"Are you sure these stairs will hold me?" asked the Tin Woodman. "I'm awfully heavy, you know."

"And so am I," said the Lion.

"Yes, I guarantee that they will hold you safely," said Micur. "I will lead the way." She seemed to float as she took the first step up the stairs.

The rest of the group followed. Halfway up, they stopped and looked around. They could see the Munchkin River and Munchkin Land, as well as the Emerald City and the Yellow Brick Road that connected them.

They climbed higher until they reached the cloud castle. The door swung open, and there stood all of Micur's family and all the people that helped to create cloud dreams and the imagination it takes to find them amongst the blue background of the sky.

Even Polychrome was there in all her brilliant rainbow colors. Everyone was so grateful that Dorothy had carried Micur out of the old mansion and into the sunlight on her own, knowing full well that the Wicked Witch would not be far behind.

After Dorothy and her friends had visited a while, Micur's father said,

"I'm afraid we must let your friends return. The wind is starting to pick up, and this castle and the stairs will soon be swept away."

Micur wiped the tears from her eyes and hugged her new friends with her tiny arms. "Just follow the stairs back down, and you will be safely on the ground. And please . . . *please* . . . watch out for the Wicked Witch."

Dorothy and Toto, the Lion, the Scarecrow, and the Tin Woodman said good-bye to Micur and all her family and friends and then slowly walked down the cloud stairs.

The blowing wind began to dissolve the castle and the stairs, so the group hurried to the ground. When they were all back on land, they watched as the stairs blew away with the wind.

They looked up into the sky, where they saw another castle in the distance and a cloud that looked just like the Tin Woodman. One cloud looked like the Lion and one like the Scarecrow, and others looked like Dorothy and Toto. And way in the far distance, they could see a lion, a tiger, and a bear.

"You see," said Dorothy, "Micur and her family and their clan continue to create new things for us. And like she said, all we need are two simple things—dreams and imagination."

The friends stared at the clouds with wonder.

The Rainbow

The Tin Woodman said, "We rescued Micur, and now she is with her family, but we are still in Never Return. How will we ever get out?"

"I don't know," Dorothy replied. "But we must find a way. Let's go back to the Silver Bridge and try again to cross it."

Her friends agreed, so they started for the bridge.

Just then, they could see the Wicked Witch scurrying along toward them. The evil witch knew that they would try to escape, so she was going to put a spell on them and make them her slaves forever.

"The Wicked Witch!" yelled the Lion.

"What shall we do?" asked the Scarecrow.

"We must hide!" Dorothy exclaimed. "Quick, let's go!" She reached to pick up Toto, but he was not at her side. She looked frantically for her little companion. Then she saw him by a berry bush, getting ready to take a bite from a green-and-purple berry.

She yelled out, "Toto, no!" But Toto was very hungry, and, to Dorothy's horror, he bit into the forbidden berry before she could stop him. He swallowed the piece of berry whole.

The Wicked Witch screamed, louder than she had ever screamed before. "Now you've done it," she cried. "Your little dog ate the wrong berry. I warned you to eat only the green-and-red ones. Now see what you have done."

And see they did. Right after Toto took his bite from the green-and-purple berry, he began to grow. He grew and grew until he was his normal size again. He towered over Dorothy, the Lion, the Scarecrow, and the Tin Woodman.

"Look, that is the secret," Dorothy said. "That is why Bekama—the Wicked Witch—warned everybody not to eat or touch the green-and-purple berries. She knew we would all grow back to our normal size."

Realizing what had happened, Dorothy and her friends ran to the bushes with the green-and-purple berries. They smashed the berries and dipped their fingers in the juice. Rapidly, they stood as tall as they had been before they entered the land of Never Return.

The Scarecrow pointed to the sky. "Look!" he said. "Look at the rainbow and clouds. It's Micur and her family, I'm sure. They are gathering a storm."

The Scarecrow's conjecture was correct. Raindrops started to pour down upon the land of Never Return. The Wicked Witch screamed for her guards, but they did not come to her aid. Without her umbrella to protect her, the raindrops began to pelt the Wicked Witch.

She screamed out, "No, not again—not now!" as she began to melt in the rain. She twirled around as she looked for a way to flee, but it was too late. She melted faster and faster; soon she was so small, you could not hear what she was screaming. After another moment, the Wicked Witch of the West had melted away, taking her evil intentions with her.

Soon the rest of her guards and all of the others who were required to obey her evil wishes began to eat the green-and-purple berries. They all quickly regained their normal size. Then they turned and thanked Dorothy, the Lion, the Scarecrow, the Tin Woodman, and even little Toto. They could now leave the land of Never Return.

They all traveled back through the forest, heading for their homes. It wasn't long before Dorothy and Toto, the Lion, the Scarecrow, and the Tin Woodman found the Yellow Brick Road, where they made their way to the Emerald City, singing and dancing as they skipped along.

"I wonder," asked the Lion, "what happened to that tall, elderly man with the mustache who lived in the old mansion? Dorothy, you said he seemed like such a good fellow. I hope he's okay."

"I am sure he is," said Dorothy, smiling broadly. "I am sure he is."

The End